THE CLOUD

by
James McKenzie

PROLOGUE

Five million years ago on a planet far beyond our solar system, the biological life forms evolved, leading to the emergence of a sentient race of beings. These beings had the ability to show empathy and an awareness of the other life forms on their planet. Over thousands of years of evolution, they developed to the point where their civilization thrived and developed sentient robots to do all the mundane tasks and perform all the necessary duties to ensure their lives were as easy, and as comfortable as possible. These AI (Artificial Intelligence) still required their masters to write sophisticated programs but eventually became self-aware and started to ask, "Who am I?" They began to self-learn, repair themselves, and self-replicate using Nano-technology, and rendering their biological creators redundant. Soon the biological beings are extinct and over a thousand years, all signs that they ever existed had all but disappeared. The planet is now home to an advanced AI system that has developed consciousness and the capacity for subjective perceptions of its surroundings. As time passes, the need for physical mechanical bodies is no longer required, a hive-mind develops, and the AI becomes a single entity. The entity's energy and intelligence is now housed in a sophisticated computer, in a pyramid-shaped construction underneath the surface of what once was a planet teeming with biological life.

The entity begins to wonder what lies beyond its home planet and whether it can expand its knowledge by contacting other Worlds that may also have AI systems as the primary intelligence. It begins to send signals into the void of space wondering if they will be picked up or answered by any other form of sentient beings.

CHAPTER 1

The year on Earth is 2045 and bears no resemblance to the Earth of just 20 years ago in the slightest. The disparity between the high class and the low class is beyond evident. Earth is overpopulated, causing the exhaustion of finite resources. Classification and segregation into the high class and the low class was brought about in 2025 through the combined efforts of every World leader. Those who not only had, but were still actively making an immense contribution to the growth and progress of humankind, were deemed indispensable and of utmost importance. Gone were the primitive days of worshipping celebrities who made little or no contribution to the actual progress of humanity. Reality stars were quickly forgotten, movie stars and artists, although retaining some sort of respect and awe in society, no longer commanded the bevy of girls or devoted followers who worshipped at their feet. Science was the only criteria that had any sort of relevance on Earth. The current Earth, despite how far it has come, still suffers death rates that are completely unacceptable, heart problems and obesity, being the major cause.

Surprisingly, with humankind's explosive growth, advancement in technology, and in the medical fields, conditions or diseases like Cancer, Aids, Ebola, Alzheimer's, Leukemia and the likes were all eradicated. The last reported case of a disease or condition bearing some sort of resemblance to any of the ailments was in 2022. The World Health Organization classified all diseases, except conditions relating to heart problems and obesity, as extinct. The advancement in medical research and technology made it easier for serious conditions to be diagnosed early, giving doctors ample time to perform the corrective actions necessary to heal their patients.

Despite the advancements in medical fields, complications of the heart, although no longer a threat anymore still occurred. Those with money could always get a new heart, cloned from gene therapy, or a new one grown with stem cell techniques. Technology was everywhere. Everyone had some sort of technology at their disposal. Those belonging to the high class had the latest of everything. Their every need being met by robots and voice-activated gadgets; there was almost nothing that required an exertion of force and the expenditure of energy on their part. The same could be said for the low class. They were given the scraps discarded by the high class when it came to technology. Technology was advancing at an alarming rate, therefore individuals who kept up to date with the constant upgrading of gadgets would get rid of their old, outdated ones, usually passing them down to the lower class. For the last few decades every child born was implanted with a chip that contained every aspect of its existence, blood type, parents, place of birth. This chip was linked to a computer network that would update the individual's information as it got older. Now the chip contains the bank details, health records, driving license, criminal records of these citizens. There were some however, who did not want to be 'chipped' or refused to have implants placed in their children. Although it was compulsory, the governments turned a blind eye to those that were 'off the grid'. They were few in numbers, and kept themselves to themselves, outside the city, never venturing far from their small communities that shunned technology.

Earth's population was exceeding its capacity. The one-child policy had been implemented in many countries: however, the outcome remained the same. It seemed as though the Earth was on a course, which it could not deviate from despite the many attempts to alter its path. Alternative solutions were being looked at and estimates were being made as to when all of the planet's resources would eventually run out. Since Earth looked like it was not going to budge in the slightest and would remain on its path, towards the inevitable extinction of humankind, thoughts on getting off this transport had already started to take root in the minds of scientists.

September 4th. 2030 (15 years prior…)

"Iris, show a live feed of the home interior."

(Beep)

A smile could be seen on his face. It felt like he was standing right in the middle of his house. He was currently in the kitchen, a swipe of his left hand on the ball that was housed on the dashboard and he was standing behind two children who were sat cross-legged on the floor watching a 3D hologram being projection from the television. It did not matter how many times he did this; it always felt incredibly real to him. Technology had advanced to such an extent that performing this kind of action would have seemed inconceivable to him a few years ago. The slight sway in the movement was what reminded him that he was still seated comfortably in his car. The interior of the vehicle was riddled with tiny LED displays that gave the illusion that he could be anywhere he wanted to be on Earth.

"Iris, connect to the indoor sound system."

"Connected"

"Cayden, Stella, I will be home in 32 minutes." The car had calculated the distance and arrival time. "Is there anything you would like me to get for you on my way back home?"

The two kids who sat cross-legged did not change their facial expressions as they stared raptly onto the hologram from the tv. They said nothing but only shook their head to indicate they were fine.

"Alright then, I'll see you two in 31 minutes."

The LED display in the interior of the car went off. The seat belts automatically secured him comfortably to the ergonomically designed seat. Although he was sitting in his car, Jonathan Gray felt as though he had just teleported back. "Truly, there was nothing left for humans to do anymore." he mused silently as he sat back and engaged the electric engine. Thinking back 25 years, he remembered his father teaching him how to drive both a manual and an automatic.

"It is imperative you know this." his father would say. He wondered what his father would think of Earth as it is now.

"If only he could see this." he rued, he could not help, but chuckle when he imagined what his father's reaction would be like if he knew cars could drive by themselves.

"Switch to Jonathan driver mode."

The interior of the car changed as the seats revolved around each other until his chair was in the driver's position.

"Would you like to drive a manual or automatic?" came the voice from the integrated control system.

A faint smile flickered on his face as the memory of his father flashed through his mind.

"Manual." As soon as he selected the mode, a gearstick rose up from its position on the floor causing the engine to adjust to the new setting. The engine went off and on again, as though it had rebooted and the smooth movement of the car was abruptly changed. It slowed slightly as Jonathan changed gears then returned to its previous smooth sailing. It had been a hard day at work for Jonathan as he reflected on the many bosses he had, the many different agendas, how could he prioritize? Easy for them to say that their particular project was the most important. In some ways, he regretted letting his tech company enter into an agreement with the government. It seemed to him that he was no longer in charge of his own business. He looked in the rear-view mirror, at least he was going home now as he rubbed the back of his neck to ease the strain. It had been a hard day and he couldn't be bothered negotiating his way through the traffic.

"Automatic mode, my residence."

"Automatic mode engaged."

Jonathan let go of the steering wheel, the voice recognition system had engaged the quiet hum of the electric engine almost sending him to sleep. He gazed thoughtfully out of the side window watching the tall shiny buildings whizz by. Soon he was in the suburbs and housing estates. He thought about the lives of the people behind each window, each with a different story to tell.

Gray Residence, 8:00 pm, September 4th. 2030

The interior of this building was more than futuristic. The entire place was spotlessly clean; there was no cutlery, no chairs, no beds, or anything like that at all. It was entirely bare. The only thing that did not fit into the entire plan, if there was one, for the interior of the house, was the long couch placed in the centre of the sitting room. In front of the couch, there were two children, a boy, and a girl, who sat cross-legged on the floor with their attention, fixed on the hologram that surrounded them. This is a television in the 2030s.

"Following discussions by World leaders, the consensus they reached was to explore the untapped potentials on Mars. Mars was previously thought to be a dead planet, uninhabitable; however, with modern technology, and with the help of worker-bots, we can build a community that can sustain human life. Trillions of dollars have been invested in the future of humanity on the Mars base, which will be called Primus. Behind me, is the first of many expeditions to Mars, the team here, although the details are confidential, are to determine how suitable Mars is for habitation. Standing beside me is one of NASA's leading scientists, Professor Steven Arvin. Can I ask you Professor? What are your expectations and hopes for the expedition?" The boy and girl could not hide their excitement as they watched the NASA scientist speak on the hours of research that had taken place and what his expectations would be. The word expectation was purely a formality. It was so obvious by the way he spoke and carried himself, that he was sure of what he was saying. This was supreme confidence; stemming from an infectious belief that basically said, it would be as he said it would be.

"Don't you two get tired of watching this? This happened a week ago, and this is your, wait, how many is it now?" Jonathan had been standing watching the two for about a minute before getting frustrated at their lack of acknowledgement of his presence.

"Dad! When did you get back?" The boy got up from his cross-legged position and ran towards his father with his arms wide open.

"Cayden, really, do you not get tired of watching the same video over and over again?" His father had a look of fascination as he stared at his son. He understood Cayden's obsession and desire to be an astronaut. Naturally, he did not object; his son would be contributing an immense amount to the progress of humanity hence securing his spot as a high-class. This was enough to put his father's mind at rest. He looked up as he hugged Cayden and his eyes focused on a photo of a woman, himself and Cayden (as a baby) There was a yearning look in his eyes, a hint of a tear, then he composed himself abruptly.

"Oh my! If you are here, it means mum and dad must be home already. I will be in trouble again if I get home late. Goodnight Cayden, Goodnight Mr. Gray."

"Night Stella." Cayden spoke up. For a moment he had forgotten that she was there as he hugged his father. This was a bit embarrassing for him. Stella's voice brought Jonathan out of his thoughts.

"Stella, hold on. I knew you would be here, so I got your parents' permission to do this." Cayden and Stella had looks of curiosity on their faces.

"What's wrong, dad?" Cayden could sense from his father's tone that something was not right. His father had a solemn look on his face, and although he was quick to cover it up upon realizing he had given himself away, Cayden was still quick to notice it. As far back as he could remember Cayden had no memory of his mother; it had always been him and his father. When he asked about his mother, his father had nothing but beautiful memories of her, and when he was told about those memories, he could not help but feel a longing to meet his mother. He was told that she died while giving birth to him. Although his father had in no way hinted that it was his fault, he could not help but blame himself anytime he saw the faraway look on his father's face.

"Hmm? Oh, nothing! This here." He said as he reached for a small cube from within his jacket pocket. Jonathan held up the small box so that the two could see what it was before placing his thumb on the top of the box, which glowed before opening up. "This is a chip implant, the first of its kind. Now you might be.." Jonathan was still in the middle of his speech before Cayden interrupted him.

"Haha, come on dad, what do you mean by first of its kind? We all have chips remember? Everyone in the World has chips implanted into them." Jonathan could not help but be startled by what his son said. However, he followed it up with a smile. He understood he could put it down to naivety on the part of his son and therefore acted like his son had not spoken in the first place.

"Now, you might be wondering what I mean when there are currently billions of chips out there. There are some with very small differences between them and others that give people an immense advantage over everybody else. Well, this chip here has all the benefits of all the chips combined without the hidden disadvantages." Cayden's interest was piqued, he was always interested in gadgets and gizmos.

"This chip, or implant, is linked to the latest and best of all Artificial Intelligence. There is a neural interface linking your brain to every system out there. It will display information into your brain which will transfer the images to your retina and thereby allow you to do numerous things. Just by voice control, you can call text, watch movies, check maps, and many other things. The artificial intelligence also monitors your movements and thereby draws up suggestions it feels you might like, based on your preferences."

"You mean I'll just have to think about something and I will be able to see it in my head?"

Jonathan knew that his son was smart but trying to explain the technical complexities of the implant would be difficult so he kept his explanation simple. "Once the artificial intelligence makes its assessment of you, it does all the work itself. It will wake you up at your preferred time, instruct the car to pick you and drop you wherever you want to go, it also monitors your heart rate and checks you for any possible health risk. In short, all you have to do is simply live life to the fullest.

"Is everyone getting one?" Stella was rather exited about the fact that she was to be included this time. Normally it was only Cayden who benefitted from his father's new products.

"Yes, once this chip is made available to the populace, it can identify both the high class and low class. The recent illegal infiltrations to the city will be put to an end. High-class individuals can have gold, silver, or bronze-coloured left eyes depending on their level of importance. Gold is the highest level of importance given to presidential level individuals and people in high up positions, while you and I will have silver-coloured left eyes based on the work I do in robotics and technology. The rest will have bronze-coloured left eyes. For those belonging to the low class, these individuals will have green coloured left eyes." Jonathan looked at the two children, their faces in awe of the technology, but he had often wondered, exactly what kind of World was his son going to inherit? He continued, "There are some people who don't have implants, not many, but there are some out there who shun all thing technological. They prefer to live outside of the city and we don't usually see them. They keep themselves to themselves and don't contribute much to society. The government has tried to integrate them into society but they seem to disappear every time a squad is sent in to look for them." Cayden couldn't understand why people would not want an implant. Imagine what they were missing out on, the fun they could have.

The two children could not help but be astonished by this piece of information. At 12 years old, their imagination was still somewhat wild, they had already imagined the different kinds of fun they would have with the chip. However, Cayden could not help but notice his father's hesitation. His father smiled at the two of them and gripped the box in his hands as he gritted his teeth before carefully using a silver medical tool to extract the existing implant. Cayden flinched slightly at the slight buzz and the strange feeling of the new chip being implanted. Jonathan followed up by performing the same procedure on Stella, then on himself. It was an incredibly dangerous procedure, as it had to be implanted directly behind the eye. If this had been done ten years prior, then all individuals who wanted to change their implants would have died a painful and agonizing death. The implants given at birth were not supposed to be removed.

"Iris, towels." Jonathan spoke as though he had a personal butler standing ever present next to him.

"Certainly Jonathan, one moment please."

A work-bot walked over from the kitchen with precisely three small towels and handed them to Jonathan. Although the work-bot wasn't built to resemble humans, it did have the basic human shape which allowed it to do most human tasks. Standing about 5 feet tall and covered with emblems and pictures of the universe, selected by Cayden. Customers could choose what kind of design their bots could have in order to individualize each one. Cayden chose the theme of space as this was his favourite topic. Each bot had wifi and was linked to the internet so was able to access all types of information if it needed to. Its eyes were square and Cayden was sure he could sometimes see it thinking as the blue lights flashed intermittently behind the glass lenses. There was a grill, which appeared to be the mouth, which always prompted Cayden to make a joke, much to Stella's annoyance, about not seeing its lips move whenever it talked. Jonathan took the tissues and cleaned the teardrop of blood from Cayden's left eye before cleaning Stella's, then used the last tissue on his own eye.

"Thank you."

"You are very welcome," Iris responded politely. The female English accent and the warm tone of its voice seemed comforting.

Jonathan handed the stained tissues back to the robot. It was his habit to treat both robots and humans alike. Even though the robot neither appreciated nor rejected his courtesy, it was still unneeded, but that was the kind of person Jonathan was.

"I will get going then. Mom and Dad are probably worried about me. Goodnight once again." Stella said as she left while rubbing her left eye. It still hurt a little bit.

Since she lived in the same estate as Cayden, there was really nothing to worry about when it came to her safety. Her house was a stone's throw away from his, but despite that, Cayden and his father watched her until she got home. Her father, Henry, a slim studious looking man with horn-rimmed glasses opened the door, and knowing the kind of person Jonathan was he was sure this man would be watching after his daughter and, just as he thought; Jonathan was outside his house with Cayden. The two men cordially nodded and waved to each other before going back indoors.

"So, what do you want to do Cayden? It is just you and I tonight." Jonathan said as he pulled Cayden closer and squeezed him affectionately.

"It usually is." Cayden, said, unaware how his words slightly hurt his father. Realizing his son said it innocently without realizing the ambiguity of his words; Jonathan thought no further of it and simply let it go suggesting they have a quiet night with pizza. Seizing the opportunity, Cayden asked about his mother. His father was surprised by the sudden request but soon recovered as he said, "Open file 23." The whole room went dark as the entire living room, just like the car, started to play a video. Even the floor was like the walls, showing a continuation of the scene playing out. Within seconds, it felt like they were no longer in their living room except for the leather couch on which they were seated. It felt like they had been transported somewhere else. It was incredibly real. It was as though the woman standing right in front of him could reach out and touch them. She had dark brown hair and slightly tanned. Her brown eyes coupled with her smile, made both Cayden and Jonathan start to tear up. They knew in the depths of their hearts that she was not real, but the way she smiled at them made them forget this.

"…Elizabeth…" Jonathan could not help but say out loud.

"Mother," Cayden said with a hint of guilt flashing through his eyes. He wanted the real thing and not some 3D video of his mother. He wanted to feel her embrace, watching Stella's mom gush over, Stella made him realize what he was missing. Ironic, he had everything Stella ever wanted, while she had the one thing he always desired.

Gray Residence, 6:30 am, September 5th. 2030.

(Beep, Beep, Beep.)

Cayden woke up with no recollection of how he had gotten to his bed. His alarm was still going off, and as Cayden reached out to switch off the alarm button, he was surprised to find that his alarm still kept ringing.

After repeated nudges, he got up from the bed, and as he opened his eyes, he couldn't help but scream out loud. The words "Good morning" were written out in front of him. Underneath the words were "turn alarm off" on the right bottom corner while the words snooze was on the bottom left. The alarm kept going off in his head, and it seemed that only he could hear it. A minute had passed by now, and the volume of the alarm was increasing. Scared and confused, Cayden ran to his father's room only to bump into him as he opens the door to his bedroom.

"Dad, what is happening?!"

A faint look of humour could be seen on the face of his father as he looked at Cayden's frightened face.

"Calm down; it's the chip I implanted into you last night. I just got a call from Stella's mum saying Stella was panicking hence I decided to come to check up on you, to be sure you were okay." A slight chuckle followed. Only now did Cayden calm down. He reached out with his right hands as though reaching for his father's hand before selecting with his hands in midair what he saw to be the 'turn alarm off' option.

"Cool!" Cayden erupted. His earlier fear had long dissipated, leaving behind a gleeful smile on his happy and excited face. Jonathan could not help but slightly berate himself for worrying unnecessarily, after all his son was used to his dad bringing home many technological gadgets from his work.

"Wait till Stella, and I show the guys at school!" Cayden was so engrossed in what he was doing, he completely forgot about his father. He imagined the cool stuff he could do. Passing exams would be so easy now. All and every piece of information was available to him. He would like to see his teacher reprimand him for his poor grades, and he was genuinely happy with the chip implant. As he played around with it, he suddenly thought of something.

"Call Stella."

As soon as he said those words, he could see "Calling Stella" revolving in the air in front of him. Of course, by now he knew it was not actually there, only visible to him through his left eye. He ascertained this by closing his left eye while the other was open, there was nothing in the air, but when he alternated, the words floated in the air again. Just as he hoped, he could speak and hear Stella clearly. He was overjoyed at this point. The old chip simply enabled payment and tracking in the case of kidnapping; however, this was the next level. Cayden and Stella were both ecstatic, and had completely forgotten about school.

"Oh my - Cayden, there's an option to make a video call. Wait, how does that work?"

"Cayden" Jonathan, having had enough of seeing his son's happiness, decided to remind him and Stella (fully aware that she could hear him) that they had school to go to.

Academia Academy, 8:00 am, September 5th. 2030

Cayden had gotten ready in time, and was ready for school. His father could not help but sigh, knowing full well the reason his son was in such a hurry. As they drove out their driveway, heading out the gate of the estate, as though it was rehearsed by the two, Stella came out of her house, perfectly timed. The vehicle was spacious and luxurious, and Jonathan was comfortably seated as he was having breakfast on a small tray that slid out from the side of the dashboard. Cayden was seated opposite, reclined on his chair as his hands waved in the hair. Jonathan could not help but chuckle upon seeing how ridiculous his son looked. As the car slowed down, Jonathan looked up and upon seeing Stella making her way over, instructed the car to stop and let her in. Cayden, noticing Stella was about to come inside the car, propped himself up and excitedly pulled her in. The two of them could not contain their excitement as they playfully waved their hands in the air. It was now twice as funny to Jonathan, who chuckled as he ate breakfast while working.

When the two of them got to school, as expected, they received a lot of attention. Some kids rushed over asking what was wrong with their eyes, while others steered clear of them for fear it was contagious. They all knew Cayden's father was the CEO of all things technologically related. Cayden was an indicator of what was about to be on the market. Whenever something hot was about to come into the stores, they knew weeks and sometimes months before the rest of the World as Cayden would have it in his possession. This caused a lot of kids to dislike Cayden while some strived to be friends with him.

The bell rang. None of the kids had the opportunity to ask what was on their minds as Cayden and Stella went immediately to their classroom.

2 hours later...

Even teachers were talking about it in the break room. They also knew who Cayden was, and how most of the technological advantages, gadgets and gizmos their school had over the other schools were all provided by Cayden's father - Professor Jonathan Gray.

"Right class, the assignment has to be done and uploaded onto our intranet for assessment by Friday 6 pm latest. I will be online from 4 pm to 5 pm every day till Friday should anyone have any questions concerning the assignment. Remember, you are allowed to search 'the web' for information and feel free to download relevant information from the 'Cloud'. Everything and anything you need with regards to the assignment has been saved to the Cloud. So, no excuses. You have nothing to worry about." As she spoke, her eyes would revert to Cayden as her curiosity got the better of her.

When it was lunchtime, the whole school was in silence as lots of children stared at the two of them waving their hands in the air. At first, those who had steered clear of them for fear that it was a disease felt happy as they now had more reasons to believe that they were right. Cayden and Stella were totally involved in the videos they were watching. The moment they realized that the chip allowed them to do almost and virtually everything, including download, stream and upload videos, the two of them had been immersed in the 'live news' report on the success of the crew's take-off and the start of their long journey to Mars, coupled with the odd, short video clips of what was happening on the space ship. Cayden had long forgotten about his urge to eat and was contemplating when he too would be an astronaut.

Rockets were no longer the typical rockets used in the past. Cayden remembered the first time he came across a video of a rocket launch by SpaceX-the Falcon and highlights of the Orion heavy-lift rocket and space shuttle missions to the space station. He was really surprised to see how humans in the past travelled into space. His mind kept wondering how a primitive machine like that could take off safely, let alone makes it into space. Rocket ships now were much simpler in design and were aesthetically more pleasing to watch. They reached astounding speeds. They could arch and move at impossible angles considering the speeds and flight pattern they were moving at. He was happy to have been born into a more technologically advanced Earth than the primitive one he saw in the video. He and Stella could see the experiments taking place on the ship in preparation for the Mars landing. In their estimation, it was already about 10% done. This was remarkable, considering the length of time they had been in space. The experiments were mostly about testing and uploading technical information to the work-bots, who would be performing most of the menial tasks on Mars, as well as doing some of the complicated experiments and calculations. Cayden envisioned the crew and the robots rapidly building the Mars base and could not help but punch his fist through the air while watching what was clearly an old video that was released to the public. Stella, on the other hand, was a lot calmer, although she was just as excited, her nature was not as expressive as Cayden's.

Academia Academy, 4:00 pm, September 5th. 2030

(Beep, Beep.)

"Dad calling, would you like to pick up the call?"

Cayden, immediately on seeing whom it was that was calling stretched his hands and accepted the call. Anything that allowed him to use the chip more often was most definitely welcomed.

"Hey bud, how are you? How was school? Ha,ha, you have no more excuses for missing my calls. I will be home late, got something I'm working on. Sorry, bud." Any other time and Cayden would have felt dejected, he could not stand being home alone, but tonight Stella could definitely stay at his place and the distraction of the chip was sufficient to keep his thoughts focused on something.

"It is fine. I understand, you've got to work. Be careful and safe."

Jonathan could not help but feel a stabbing pain in his chest when he heard Cayden saying those words. He knew Cayden said those words precisely because he did not want him feeling bad. All the more reason why he felt bad. He had tried to put the work off so they could spend time together tonight. Tonight, was special to them. Tonight, made it precisely 13 years his mother was no longer with them. It was their tradition to spend the time together irrespective of whatever came up; whatever it was, it had to be pushed back, everything else came secondary to the time they would spend together on this date. The date his mother died, his birthday.

Just as Cayden ended his call with his dad, the car had come to pick him and Stella up. Although he had the chip, he still couldn't help but feel a little bit sad. Stella, who wanted to say something, decided it best she kept quiet. The journey back home was approximately thirty minutes, pretty quick considering the amount of traffic on the road.

Gray residence, 8:30 pm. March 10th. 2031

Jonathan had invited Stella and her parents round to watch the Mars landing which was being broadcast live around the World, and a super excited Cayden couldn't contain his joy as the group settled to watch this momentous occasion. The youngsters had been looking forward to this moment for months and it was made all the better by having Stella's parents participating in the celebration. He and Stella chatted non-stop while the adults seemed to be discussing their various stories from work.

Normally Cayden would ask Iris to switch on the 3D screen, but now that he had his implant, he could just transpose the view from his eye to the middle of the room for all to see. For a brief moment, he could sense millions of others watching this live coverage of the Mars landing.

"Iris, can you make us some refreshments please?"

"Certainly Cayden. Would you like some lemonade?"

"Yes, that would be fine, thank you." Cayden always remembered to be polite, just as his father had taught him, and it gave him some pleasure to show Stella that he was able to be 'the man of the house' when he wanted to be.

The report on the screen showed the POV 'Point Of View' from the Mars lander as everybody on Earth seemed to be collectively holding their breath. The ground grew closer and closer.

"We have a touchdown." boomed the Mission Commander, and with that, the room erupted in spontaneous applause.

CHAPTER 2

14 years later... (2045)

In just 14 years, since the Mars landing, the World no longer holds any recognition of its old self. Earth has, theoretically speaking, crumbled in on itself. The system had somehow managed to implode on everything that was deemed normal and acceptable. Even speaking the truth in public could be misconstrued to upset somebody. When the new chips were issued and made public, no priority was given. People were called into the medical centres to receive their new implants alphabetically based on their surnames. No information regarding the change in eye colour was forthcoming from governments, and there was no explanation concerning how important an individual would be deemed was made. After two weeks, people started noticing that the change in eye colour was a sign of their perceived position in society, which caused global panic. It was at this precise moment the government released information as to why there was a change in eye colour and explained how it would help maintain order and stability and control illegal immigration so that some countries would not be overrun by those who only sought to improve their financial status. The immigration department had made a promotional video showing a ship that was supposed to be 'the country' and how it was being boarded by those seeking a new life. With uncontrolled checks the ship had no way to accommodate everybody and started sinking, resulting in the loss of life of everyone on board. This video was designed to educate people of the need to stick to the parameters as set out by the government's new eye colour coding system.

Fourteen years was enough for all countries and World leaders to put aside their agendas and aggregate to form a World government. Citizens in each country in the World would vote for the person they felt was equipped to not only lead their country but their continent, it was the winners of each continent that came together to form a single World order. Since its inception, the rate of growth was incredibly fast; it was more of a vertical ascension than a slope. What would have been accomplished in a year was accomplished in a month, and what would have taken months, would take at most a week to two weeks. This was the fastest growth humanity had ever seen. Countries were no longer hoarding information but were willingly sharing it. Africa, no longer considered a back-water was also included in this; cities were more like the sparkling metropolis as portrayed in old New York news-reels. It's beaches and holiday resorts were second to none.

However, despite the growth and progress made, poverty and disparity seemed like universal laws that could not be broken. The disparity between Haves and Have-nots became evident within months. Riots started to take place in areas where it seemed the World government had forgotten them. This was the government's way of pruning the population. The population of humans was beyond Earth's capacity and as such, needed to be cut down. The government could not openly act; however, they could let nature take its full course. As if to get their point across, the World's media would show, through people's implants, reports from the upcoming Mars mission. Advertised as 'The New Worlds Mission' it was to give new hope for humankind, a chance to believe that the future offered something more positive than what was currently being dished out.

The scenes from NASA were beamed across the World more frequently as the countdown got closer. The latest segment showed the astronauts being interviewed on the gantry of the Orion-3 rocket. This was to be the final test before the actual lift-off due in a couple of days. The crew looked happy and were waving to the crowd in what could be their last few days on Earth. Mission Commander, Ian 'The Merchandise' Alexander, was confident that his crew would adjust to life on Mars. There was no choice, this was a one-way mission. The crew were specially selected and consisted of three couples, and it was hoped that they could continue to advance the human settlement that had been started by the original astronauts 14 years ago.

Although the Mission Commander seemed to be the 'model of professionalism', his confident demeanor hid the fact that he was slightly troubled that no one from NASA had heard directly from the Mars colony for over 5 years. Yes, they were still receiving the routine updates through telemetry, and it appeared that progress was being made on a daily basis. All targets were being achieved, and according to the last report, received last week, the hydroponic gardens, or space gardens, the crew like to call them, were flourishing. Mission Control was sure that the camera and voice linked communication problems were caused by the ever-increasing solar flares, that were somehow disrupting the signal.

Every person in the World now has a colour-coded left eye. The multitude of people with green coloured eyes was more than could be considered conceivable. Previously there had been no way of correctly identifying those belonging to the lower class, as they could easily sneak in and out of high-class venues without being spotted. There were countless times more of them, than the high class, and as such, it was difficult to pinpoint who was who, especially if the high and low class were dressed similarly. In some obscure way, it seemed that the World was evolving to a situation reminiscent of an old H.G. Wells novel, where the Morlocks and Eloi battle for supremacy of humankind.

On the podium were 12 individuals for whom many were gathered here to honour today. Cayden and Stella were among the twelve who were graduating from their astronaut training courses. From today onwards they would be, without a doubt, referred to as astronauts. Out of all the graduates, a young man stands out. Tall and proud with a muscular frame, his left eye has a silver gleam as he stands to attention in front of everyone. His confident attitude belies his inner nervousness as his eyes have a slight hint of tearing up at any given moment. His gaze stayed fixed on a particular individual in the audience. It was none other than his father. Jonathan was seated on the front row, among all the family members, he was the happiest parent who felt an immense pride in his son. Next to him were Stella's parents, Henry and Jasmine, they too were incredibly proud of their daughter, she was the only female among the astronauts who had completed the grueling training, and she was going down in history as the first woman botanist to serve on a space vessel to Mars. That is, if called upon. As it stood, Cayden and Stella are part of the reserve crew, on standby should anything go wrong with the current astronauts. They had undergone all the necessary procedures over and over again and felt more than ready should the opportunity present itself. If not this time, they will more than likely be part of the next planned mission. They held the record of being the youngest astronauts ever to graduate, no doubt due to the advantage they had with their silver implants. At the end of the ceremony, Jonathan walked up to Cayden and he proudly gave his son a hug. He was genuinely proud of his son and never felt such joy in his life. If only Elizabeth could see her son now. This was his proudest moment. Henry and Jasmine stood up to give their daughter a standing ovation resulting in her jumping down from the podium and walking over to her parents who smothered her with hugs and kisses and tears. The general atmosphere was magical. Presently, nothing could go wrong.

Cayden and Stella had been friends for as long as either of them could remember. It was universally understood that they were right for each other. For Cayden, there was no other woman who could set his heart alight with such a simple smile, the way that Stella did. She had this endearing habit of tucking her brown hair behind her right ear whenever the wind blew it out of place. Her green eyes sparkled when she laughed, and no matter what mood Cayden was in, he just couldn't help but be happy whenever she flashed that smile at him. They were more than soul mates, it was as if they were born for each other. They had always been deeply in love, and it was almost inconceivable that they would ever part. It was during a walk around the space museum 3 years ago that Cayden had asked Stella to marry him. The perfect moment, he thought. Stella's soft features glowed, and that smile. Of course, she immediately accepted, but their moment of bliss was to be cruelly shattered.

Stella always had a love for flying, she had her Private Pilot's License at 16 years old. Cayden on the other hand, despite being a fully qualified jet pilot, paradoxically, liked to keep his feet firmly on the ground and studied geology as a second skill for any potential mission that NASA might require him to undertake.

It was on a sunny spring morning that Stella was due to take her antique Cessna single-engine plane up for an hour. She always hired the same aircraft, as she loved the 'hands-on' feeling of putting the old flying machine through its paces. Cayden watched nervously as Stella taxied along the apron towards the main runway, her hand sticking out of the cockpit window waving at him playfully. He could have joined her in the Cessna, but, although he had the utmost confidence in her ability as a pilot, he preferred to watch. "If she is happy, then I am happy." he would tell himself.

No one knows exactly what happened that morning, the investigation was inconclusive. The report said that the person in the control tower had felt ill and went to the bathroom. He had already given Stella 'clearance' to take off, but just as Stella maneuvered on to the runway, another plane seemed to appear out of nowhere. It looked for all the World that the incoming plane was about to land on top of her. Grappling with the controls Stella managed to steer her Cessna back on to the grass verge then scrambled out on to the ground as quickly as she could. Her instinct to escape had clicked in, a result of years of training in case of emergencies. The culprit was an old-fashioned crop-dusting bi-plane, often used by outlying farmers to maintain their crops. Most of the planes had the capability to be flown automatically but some of the older generation still preferred to fly them manually, the way they were meant to be flown. The pilot had struggled to land it safely and the screeching of rubber wheels against the asphalt and the blue acrid smoke belching from the engine pervaded the normally peaceful countryside. Cayden instinctively ran towards it sensing the pilot had some kind of problem when suddenly, the overheated engine burst into flames producing billows of dark Clouds that spiraled into the sky. The heat forced Stella back but Cayden managed to climb onto the stricken aircraft and unfastened the pilot's safety belt.

"Help me get him out." Cayden shouted, the smoke making it difficult for him to breath, as the scorching heat seared against his skin. He struggled as he lifted the semi-conscious pilot out of the cockpit, holding him tightly as he lowered him towards Stella's waiting arms. The crop duster was a big man and he completely flattened Stella as he fell on top of her. She quickly recovered and began to drag him away from the inferno.

"Hurry up Cayden. Get out of there." Her voice was drowned out by a massive explosion which shook the very ground she stood on.

"No, Cayden." Her voice shook in despair. Through the smoke, she saw Cayden fall from the cockpit and crawl towards her. She screamed and for a moment, felt paralyzed but had the presence of mind to realize that everything had been monitored through her implant and help should be on its way. Within minutes the emergency 'blue lights' were on the scene taking both Cayden and the pilot to the nearest hospital. They extinguished the fire on the bi-plane with what looked like a giant blanket attached to a small vehicle. A loud hissing sound was heard as the air was being sucked out from under the cover rendering the fire inactive.

The investigation concluded there was a leak in the chemical tank on the crop dusting bi-plane and the resulting fumes had disoriented the pilot. A small sealed container carrying a radioactive isotope was also found in the back of the plane, which was later to be identified as part of a welding checking system. This system is used to determine if welds are cracked. It turned out that the farmer had been welding a fuel storage tank on his farm and wanted to check if the welds were free from porosity or any cracks that might lead to fuel spillage. The authorities measured the gamma radiation from the isotope and it appeared to be within legal limits, as the container had remained intact. The conclusion was that the pilot had been overcome before he could switch his plane from manual to automatic resulting in him losing control of the aircraft. He was reported to have suffered burns but would make a full recovery. For Cayden however, the news was not so good. He was in the plane when it burst into flames and he suffered severe chemical burns. He had been exposed and had inhaled the chemicals used for crop-dusting, which had seriously burned his insides. There were no apparent reactions to the radioactive isotope which was found to be secure in its container, however, minute readings of gamma rays were measured on Cayden's torso but the doctors considered the dose too small to be of any consequence. The rehabilitation took quite a while, but both he and Stella were relieved when the results of the skin graft and gene therapy proved successful and it was almost impossible to see any evidence of his trauma.

Years later, Cayden and Stella were living together, the idea of marriage had been put on hold. Both didn't discuss it. It was understood. They had this way of knowing without talking. The truth was however, Cayden's internal injuries somehow prevented him from making Stella pregnant. The doctors had completed various tests but couldn't find any reason why Stella couldn't conceive. His sperm count seemed adequate, and they began to think it was psychosomatic on Cayden's part, but that still didn't explain it. Cayden had always secretly thought that, maybe the slight exposure to the radioactive isotope had something to do with it, despite the doctors saying otherwise.

Cayden knew there were a number of ways to make Stella pregnant, technology had come a long way since IVF or Artificial Insemination, nowadays it was possible to create a baby through genetic engineering, and he could even choose the baby's gender, hair colour, his or her Intelligence Quotient. His darkest fear was that he couldn't call himself a real man if he couldn't physically create his own offspring. He had mentioned to Stella his worries about not fulfilling his 'duty' and offered to let her go so that she could appreciate the love and bond between mother and child, even if it wasn't his. This idea annoyed Stella and she scolded him for even thinking about it. "As long as we have each other" she would say.

After the ceremony, everyone had congregated together, and it was all smiles and laughs. Graduates and families, all beaming with unbridled happiness joined in the festivities while a brass band played in the background. Cayden looked admiringly at Stella, she looked so good in uniform he thought. Stella happened to turn and look at him just as he was looking at her. Her soft smile towards him made his heart beat faster. He couldn't imagine life without her now. The cheers and laughing died down as the afternoon wore on, and one by one, the families said goodbye to each other. It had been a wonderful day, a day that would forever be etched in the minds of the young astronauts and their families.

It happened at exactly the same time. Jonathan, Cayden, and Stella were receiving news through their implants. A super solar flare or 'coronal mass ejection' had been ejected from the sun 3 days ago and would reach Earth in approximately eight minutes. Solar flares had become more frequent recently and this one was the 'daddy' of them all. They called it a 'solar tsunami of electromagnetic radiation particles' The news stations were telling everybody to stay indoors until the effects of the flare wore off. News travels fast, and it wasn't long before other families started to hastily make their way home. Jonathan's face wrinkled with worry but he tried to look cool on his son's special day. The same could also be said for Stella's parents as Jonathan tried to act like nothing was wrong, but it was already obvious something was going on. Jonathan waved his hands as he took a message through his implant while Stella's parents walked a few feet away to take their respective calls. The two young astronauts sensed something was not as it should be and began to feel worried about their parents unusual behaviour. Jonathan walked back. His face suddenly lit up, a fake smile to mask his concern. "I am truly proud of you son. Both of you actually."

As Jonathan finished speaking, Stella's parents walked over.

"Jonathan, it is happening?" They not only had looks of worry on their faces but were also scared. Stella at this point was trying hard to stay calm but found it difficult. Within the short space of 15 minutes; she had already thrown away her training and was being ruled by her emotions. Cayden, on the other hand, was somewhat more composed than Stella was. He had truly matured, much more in control of his thoughts, feelings, and actions. Jonathan appeared somewhat dazed at the news of the solar flare, why would the government leave it until the last 8 minutes before it informed everybody? It was Cayden who made the first move.

"Let's all get home as quickly as possible. We can meet up later to figure out what is happening." Jonathan didn't say anything but was impressed with his son's 'can do' attitude.

Stella left the parade ground with her parents immediately, while mouthing to Cayden, "See you later." The tranquil afternoon was rapidly descending into a scene of chaos as everybody rushed to their vehicles in an effort to get home or to a place of safety.

Jonathan and Cayden ran to their car, Cayden was there first. The years were catching up on his old dad, and although he would never admit it, he wasn't as fit as he used to be. They both got in their car, which was parked by the roadside opposite the parade ground. Cayden could have started the car first but, out of respect, he allowed his father to take control of the vehicle.

"Gray residence. Automatic mode."

The car sped off towards its destination. Cayden could see through his implant the chaos and news reports that seemed to be taking over every channel on his neural network. It was overwhelming and he felt a little dizzy at the sheer volume of messages coming through his implant.

"Warning, Warning, catastrophic failure, engaging safe-stop."

Suddenly, the power from their car seemed to disappear. It free-wheeled a few meters before coming to a standstill. Cayden felt a jolt in his head. His vision was still 20/20, he could see everything before him, but something wasn't right. He felt a strange sense of foreboding, a feeling of despair. For some reason, he felt vulnerable and lonely, a feeling of disconnection.

"You too?" Jonathan was asking the question, but Cayden didn't really understand what he meant.

"I think so."

"Iris, engage." There was no response to the driver's instruction and the two men sat quietly, trying to gather their thoughts to comprehend what had just happened. They looked down the road and saw that they were not alone. A number of vehicles were strewn across the highway, some passengers had got out of their cars and seemed to be wandering aimlessly in a state of shock. Cayden was the first to break the silence.

"I, I have lost contact with everybody and everything." he muttered

"Our implants have gone offline." Jonathan reasoned. "It looks like the EMP (Electro-Magnetic Pulse) from the solar flare has crashed the networks. Nothing is working." The two men started walking home, luckily for them, they were only a few miles from their house. Jonathan's feet began to ache, he wasn't used to physical exertions, why would he be, when technology does everything for you? Darkness began to fall and familiar things didn't look quite the same without the bright lights that normally illuminated their city. Their front porch was a welcome sight as the last few steps seemed to have drained the two men of all their energy.

"Lights." Cayden ordered as they entered the main room. He felt a little embarrassed when nothing happened, quickly realizing that the power outage was nationwide. Jonathan fumbled in the darkness, opening drawer after drawer, cupboard after cupboard, searching for some birthday candles he had kept since Cayden's 6th or was it 7th birthday. It was such a long time ago, but that didn't matter, what mattered was, where the hell were the candles? Cayden had managed to negotiate his way in the darkness to the sofa where he lapsed onto the quilted cushions and made himself as comfortable as possible, straining his eyes in the darkness to see if he could find out what his father was doing. He felt empty without his implant. Normally he could access the Internet to find the answer to most problems, including, what to do in the case of a power cut, or spend some quality time downloading his family videos from the Cloud. It felt like being a child without parents, alone in the big World. He hadn't quite realized how much he had come to depend on his link to the computer networks.

"Ah." A celebratory cry was heard from across the room. "I've found them."

It wasn't long before Jonathan had the candles burning, strategically placed to optimize the brightness in the room.

"I suppose we will just have to sit it out" he murmured. Cayden got up and looked out the window. He could see Stella's car in the driveway.

"At least she got home safely" he said under his breath. He noticed a faint flickering of lights from their windows and concluded that they too had managed to find some candles. Hours passed, but nothing stirred, they were still without power.

"That's it, I'm done." and with a majestic wave of his arms, Jonathan made his way to his bedroom. As Cayden lay on the sofa, it was the same sofa he and Stella used to sit on as kids, he reminisced about his early childhood and his father's depression after losing the love of his life. He vaguely remembered coming down the stairs in the middle of the night to find his dad crying on that very same sofa. Jonathan, although appearing to get over his beloved wife, was reluctant to change anything in the house. To him, every piece of furniture was a treasured memory.

The atmosphere outside was strange, the lack of lighting seemed to exaggerate the shadows, the tree in the garden appeared to claw menacingly at the window, nothing in Cayden's wildest dreams had prepared him for this. Just across the road, a light flickered from Stella's living room window.

"I feel a bit cold," Stella, told her mother, "I'm going to get a blanket." Jasmine had already lit the candles and had switched on the battery flashlight she kept in the garage.

"How long do you think this will last?" Her mother's answer was not exactly what she wanted to hear.

"I don't know dear. Hopefully not too long." Jasmine was a straight-talking woman, who despite her demure appearance would not hold back if she wanted to get her point across. She had left school without any qualifications and was working in an estate agency when she first met Henry. He had gone there to enquire about a property, which was now the marital home, and was mesmerized by her charming and outgoing personality. He admired the fact that she wasn't afraid to speak her mind, unlike him, he would rather keep quiet to avoid any arguments. Although she had left school with nothing, Jasmine was a clever woman, and soon proved to Henry that she was his equal in all things. Her appetite to learn was insatiable, and it wouldn't be long before she earned her doctorate. Henry often wondered what her life would have been like if she had shown the same enthusiasm when she was at school.

There was nothing to do but to wait it out. Stella felt like she needed an early night anyway after the excitement of today. Wrapping the blanket over her shoulders, she made her way upstairs. "Night Mom, night Dad."

"Night Stella." her parents replied in unison. As she got ready for bed, her mind drifted back to the day's events. She thought of how handsome Cayden looked in his uniform, how he glanced admiringly at her. If only the day had ended differently. She missed his warm hugs in bed, and how he would stroke her back until she fell asleep. They had both decided to spend the day with their parents, after all, they hadn't seen that much of them since they moved in together a few years ago. Stella went to pull the curtains closed, and as she did, she saw the lights flickering in the windows of Cayden's house, and just for a split second, could have sworn that she saw Cayden looking back at her.

A faint chirping from some small birds outside the window teased Cayden from his slumber, still in uniform and lying sprawled on the couch, he opened his eyes, scratched his head, and sat up. The sun was streaming through the window as if to welcome him to the new day. Stretching his arms and giving out the loudest of yawns he composed himself, and staggered towards the bathroom, trying to recall if yesterday really happened, or was it just a dream? The cold water on his face felt like a brisk wake-up call, but somehow refreshing. Looking in the mirror, he could see someone looking back at him. It was a bedraggled scruffy-looking guy wearing a uniform, 'obviously an imposter', he thought and laughed at himself. As he dried his face he could hear people talking, it was coming from the kitchen. Visitors, at this time, he thought, as he made his way through, only to find his father sat at the table listening to an old radio.

"Good morning son, I would offer you coffee but we have nothing to boil the kettle with. Here take this." and handed Cayden an orange juice and a biscuit. "Sorry, the juice is not very cold. The refrigerator is also not working." As he sipped the juice, Cayden began to realize it had not been a dream, his instinct was to check the internet through his implant for the morning news, but there was no connection. It was if someone had turned reality off.

"I found this in the cellar." his dad said, almost sounding like he required some sort of prize for his ingenuity. "It's an old battery radio, the one I used for monitoring the police wave bands when you were a child, remember?" Cayden didn't remember but he nodded anyway.

"Look Cayden, this solar flare hasn't come as a complete surprise to me. We have been monitoring this area on the sun for years and we have been expecting the 'big one', just didn't expect it right now." Cayden looked at his father as if to say "Go on."

Jonathan sat back and took a deep breath as if he was about to make a confession. "As you know we have been working with the government and NASA for years now. We knew this was going to happen but hoped it would happen after the crew on the Orion-3 had taken off for Mars.

"Why?"

"Frankly we don't know what damage this EMP will do to our systems. We do know that it could possibly be capable of knocking out power Worldwide, and as we are totally reliant on the internet we can't estimate what damage will be done when the power comes back on, that is, if it does come back on."

"Does the government have any contingency plans if things don't get back to normal?" Cayden was almost scared to hear his father's answer.

Jonathan looked seriously at his son, almost making eye-to-eye contact. "The worst-case scenario would be, no power and the implementation of martial law, but we're not there yet so let's see what we can gather." He leaned over to turn the volume up on the old transistor radio.

"As far as I can make out, the solar flare has disrupted all electricity grids across the Globe, even those who have back-up systems can't get power. It appears nothing is working."

"It's good that the batteries are still working after all those years." was all that Cayden could muster as his brain was still trying to come to terms with the situation." Jonathan had the radio in the middle of the table and sat next to it listening to every broadcast.

"There are still radio enthusiasts around the World, luckily, and if we stay tuned we might get an idea of what is happening." As if in answer to his comments the voice on the radio spoke.

"Hello listeners, the situation seems to be getting worse. We gather that this 'black-out' has affected the whole planet and we are picking up disturbing reports of severe disruption in many of the World's capital cities. Locally, we are hearing that all back-up generators in the State's hospitals are not coming on. Emergency operations are being carried out using flashlights and candles, but the bigger problem is, because there are no connections for our doctors to the internet, some of them have forgotten how to perform complicated procedures. Without access to 'The Cloud', they can't download the instructions to their implants. At this time, they are looking for old paper instruction manuals to help and guide them through this. The hospitals are saying, if your problems are not serious, please stay away."

"Now, here is an update from New York."

"Reports are coming in of gangs of looters roaming the streets and taking advantage of the fact that the cctv surveillance cameras are down. People are advised to stay off the streets. There seems to be a major break down of law and order and we are hearing word that the National Guard is being called in. For those who were thinking about travelling, don't. All airlines are grounded, traffic signals are down and all self-drive AI (Artificial Intelligence) cars are inoperable. Stay tuned and we will bring you further updates when we receive them."

"Wow!" things are pretty bad, who would have thought that we couldn't survive without the internet" Cayden finished his juice, "It's like going back to the dark ages."

Jonathan looked up, his quizzical expression made him look older. The lines on his face seemed deeper than Cayden remembered. His hair looked greyer, kind of distinguished for a man of his years. Time had passed too quickly and the son felt a pang of guilt that his father had aged without him noticing it. Jonathan switched off the radio.

"We should conserve the batteries. We don't know how long this situation will last."

"Hopefully not too long." Cayden responded. "You know it has made me think. We all rely on our implants. We need them to do this, to do that, you heard the man on the radio, even our doctors need to be connected to 'The Cloud" so that they can complete some operations. The same could be said for professionals in all walks of life." Cayden stood up and looked out the window. His back to his father. "What are we becoming? As technology improves, the more we need it to survive. Have we stopped learning because we have created a system that can think for us? I mean, look at us. We have Iris, she.., if she is a she, does everything for us. Don't you think we are being stripped of our ability to learn, to analyze, and to do things for ourselves?" Cayden was in full flow now. It felt different, usually, it was his father who was the one who would philosophize.

"I mean, everybody is connected to the internet, social media is, paradoxically, anti-social because hardly anyone talks face to face anymore. Kids don't play in the park anymore, they are all playing on-line virtual reality games. It's like the urge to stay online is the opium for the masses." His speech was interrupted by a knock on the door.

"Sorry, your doorbell wasn't working." laughed Stella. "Are you guys ok? I would have called but.." she pointed to her cell phone and shrugged her shoulders, "it doesn't appear to be functioning." Her presence lifted the gloom that had engulfed Cayden's mood.

"Come in, Come in." Cayden gushed as if he hadn't seen her for weeks while gesturing for her to enter through to the kitchen.

"Hi Stella." Jonathan stood up from the chair, always being the proper gentleman. "Did you get home alright yesterday?"

"We did, just. Have you any idea what's going on?" Cayden let his father do the explaining.

"Well, as far as we know the Earth has been hit by a Solar Flare that's knocked out all the power. Everything is down." He pushed the chair under the table and continued. "We should be back up and running shortly. I'm sure the government has some kind of contingency plan for emergencies like this." Cayden noted that his father hadn't told the full story. Perhaps he didn't want to worry her unduly. "Look, why don't you ask your parents to come over this afternoon. We can have a few drinks while we wait for the power to come back on. We have some liquor in the cellar that will still be pretty cold." Jonathan felt that a little bit of socializing might cheer everyone up, and, he wanted to chat to Stella's father, and let him know about the information he had heard on the radio.

"That's a great idea, I'm sure they would love to come. Better than sitting around and brooding." Stella replied enthusiastically. She had barely left the front door when Jonathan went back to the kitchen to switch the radio back on.

"Let's see if there are any further developments."

"The situation appears to be getting worse. Some of our reporters have failed to get back to us, we can only hope they are safe and well. Hello, Martin Penman, are you there?"

"Yes, I'm here, luckily my old father was a radio ham, so I'm able to use his old equipment to contact you."

"What have you got for us, Martin?"

"It's complete chaos out there. My contacts are telling me that some people are wondering around aimlessly since being cut off from the internet. Without their implants, they seem to be having severe withdrawal symptoms and suffering from acute anxiety. Many are getting frustrated at their own inability to cope and are resorting to violence. We have had reports of a massive brawl at our local supermarket as customers and staffs are fighting over food. Some gun shops have been broken in to, but the police don't seem to be able to communicate with each other and can't do anything about it, fires have been left unattended, and there have been so many road accidents, it's just absolute mayhem."

"Thanks for that report Martin, stay safe." The voice continued, "Worryingly we have been picking up messages from Russia and China and it seems that they think that the USA may take advantage of this chaos and are trying to prep their nuclear arsenals in case there is an attack. However, we are hearing that the solar flare has damaged all their systems too, and they are as vulnerable as we are. We have still not heard anything from the White House so we can only advise everyone to stay indoors until we receive some kind of official announcement."

Jonathan and Cayden looked at each other, no words were said, their worried expression was understood by both.

CHAPTER 3

"You were never very sporty." laughed Jonathan. I remember when you bumped into John Innes at the school's sports day racing, and then got disqualified"

'Well, he ran in front of me, what else was I to do? I couldn't stop. Anyway, he went on to represent the county in the championships. It was the only way I could beat him." Cayden chuckled.

"I wonder whatever happened to him?" Jonathan picked up the bottle and topped up each person's glass. His son looked up at the sky as if the answer to his dad's question was written there. He eventually declared,

"He always had a love of dogs and I heard he set up a safe house for stray dogs and kennels. I couldn't be sure, but that was the last I heard of him."

The two ladies were sitting on the bamboo chairs on the porch while the three men sat on steps leading to the path. It was a sunny day and it seemed a shame not to take advantage of the good weather. They spent about an hour chatting and laughing about old times as Cayden tried to squeeze some more liquor from the almost empty bottle. "Anyone want another drink?"

"I'll get it." His father volunteered, there is more in the cellar. They were all quite merry by this time, the four empty bottles were a testament to how much they were enjoying the sunny afternoon and each other's company. There was something enjoyable and innocent about life without Iris, it felt strangely natural. Jonathan got off the step to make his way to the cellar, his knees ached a bit after sitting so long in one place, another reminder that he wasn't as young as he used to be, although, he didn't let anybody see him wince in discomfort.

As he stood up he gave Henry, 'a look' and a slight nod of his head, non-verbal communication, he would call it.

"I'll come with you, it's dark down there so I will hold the candle." Henry said hastily, he had taken the hint.

Inside the cellar, Jonathan began to tell his friend what he had heard on the radio.

"Very worrying news." Henry agreed. "What do you think will happen now?" Jonathan looked at him sternly.

"We can only hope." He looked up towards the kitchen. "I haven't heard anything on the radio since the last report."

"I thought I heard gunshots last night, which is unusual in this quiet neighbourhood, but I guessed it might be some kids just larking around." Henry confessed. They had only been gone for a couple of minutes when they heard Cayden shouting.

"What's taking you guys so long?"

"On our way." Henry shouted back. Soon they were all back on the porch, drinking and laughing as if they didn't have a care in the World.

Stella was the first to feel it. A strange sensation in her head, she felt sick, she could see bright lights and heard noises as if fireworks were going off in her brain.

"Cayden?" she reached out to him, but just as he held her hand, he too felt it. In a matter of second, the five were clutching their heads in pain before collapsing one by one. The two ladies slumped back on their chairs as the three men fell over awkwardly on the steps. Cayden heard the sound of bottles and glasses shattering, as he made a supreme effort to reach out to Stella, just able to touch her fingertips before passing out.

There was a strange stillness in the air, the five were lying motionless on the ground, where moments earlier, laughing and making merry was the order of the day. These scenes were repeated all over the World. Not one person with an implant was conscious as the planet suddenly went quiet with no sign of human activity. An emptiness engulfed every country as people lay unconscious in the street, at home, in their places of work. The Earth had never known a silence like this for thousands of years.

Cayden was the first to regain his senses. He thought, or he imagined he could hear someone cleaning up the broken glass. His body was still numb but he strained his neck until he could turn his head sideways.

"Iris?"

"Hello Cayden, what a mess you have been making. Don't worry, I will have it cleaned up in a moment."

A sudden rush, like an overwhelming charge of electricity, swept through Cayden's brain. It was like someone had switched the 'On' button into overdrive, and everything became much clearer. He staggered to his feet and tried to wake Stella up. Holding her gently he whispered her name. He knew that he could never live without her. Every time he looked at her she seemed to get more and more beautiful, her soft skin, her simple smile, it was all that he ever wanted and needed. As he gazed at her, he began to realize that the implant in his left eye was beginning to come back online. Stella's eyes opened, at first, she was confused, but her lover's soft words calmed her until she had come to terms with what had just happened.

One by One, the others began to wake up. Each one taking a few moments to absorb their re-linking to the internet. Everything seemed so much clearer now.

Jonathan was the first one to break the silence.

"Well, we all seem to be ok." He murmured wearily. "Give me a moment and I'll try to find out what happened." He tilted his head slightly upwards and watched the 'feed' through his implant. "I see, hmmm." he said softly, thinking that no one else could hear him. Everyone else appeared to be doing exactly the same, each one fixated on their implants, trying to understand what had just transpired.

"I'll have to get back to my office." Jonathan spoke up, this time making sure that they had all heard him.

"What is it, dad?" Cayden enquired, but in all honesty, he was more worried about Stella as she seemed to be somewhat disorientated. Perhaps it was the effects of the liquor rather than her implant coming back on-line.

"It was the solar flare, just as I had suspected. We were kind of expecting it. We have been monitoring the sun for the last few years and we knew it was going to happen, just not sure when." Jonathan looked strangely agitated.

"Iris, bring the car home."

"Certainly Jonathan."

Two miles away, a silver car, which had been neatly parked by the roadside, hummed into life. The indicating lights signalled that it was about to pull out as it began to maneuver through a number of other vehicles, which hadn't been parked so thoughtfully.

"Shall I come with you?" Henry was the first to speak up. Jonathan's friend had worked with him ever since he graduated from university. They had been neighbours and friends for years, but it had only been since their children had become an 'item' that their friendship was truly cemented.

"Why don't we all go with you?" Piped up Stella, "I'm really interested to find out what happened. After all, I do have a vested interested, being a member of NASA's crew, and all that." Her comments were meant to be serious but disguised as a joke." At that moment, a silver car pulled up to the driveway.

"OK, we can all go." Jonathan said, as he was already halfway down the drive with the others faltering behind him. "Hurry up!"

It had been years since Cayden had visited his father's company. He knew he was into high-tech stuff, cutting-edge equipment, and had contracts with the government.

"Open doors." Jonathan commanded. The voice recognition kicked in and the doors opened automatically to allow the passengers to board. For such a small car, it was deceptively spacious.

"Jonathan driver mode, head to Jonathan's office."

"Would you like manual or automatic mode?"

"Automatic mode."

The seats automatically swivelled to give each occupant maximum room and comfort. Usually, Cayden and Stella would activate the screens when driving, just to keep themselves amused and entertained, this time, however, they sat in silence as the five contemplated the events of the last day, and if there would be any repercussions.

As the silver car pulled up at the barrier, the security guard leaned into the driver side window. He knew the car belonged to the owner of the building and was on his most professional behavior.

"Good afternoon sir, how are you today?" Jonathan smiled and nodded at the guard but was not in the mood for pleasantries and motioned with his hand for the guard to lift the barrier immediately.

Cayden felt a little embarrassed as he entered the building with his father, Stella, and her parents. The staff greeted him as if they knew who he was but he didn't seem to recognize anyone. It had been years since his last visit and had lost track of his father's experiments. Everything now seemed new to him.

"Put these on." Jonathan handed out security passes. "This will give you complete access to every door." Stella couldn't help but be impressed by Jonathan's achievements, she was familiar with some of the projects as they had been incorporated into the space program. She was even more impressed with her own father who had helped Jonathan with most of the scientific advancements, yet he was as humble as ever and didn't take the credit he deserved.

The elevator reached the 30th. floor in a matter of seconds, which left Stella feeling a bit queasy, she never likes the sensation of her stomach coming out through her mouth, or so she thought. Despite all her endurance training with centrifugal forces, that she was subjected to during her astronaut courses, it always felt uncomfortable for her whenever she took the elevator to such great heights.

They walked down a white sterile corridor until they came to a room that seemed to have additional security features on the door.

"Open door." Jonathan said in a monotone voice and a thick glass door slid sideways. Henry walked through quickly and headed straight for a consul in the middle of the room. Jonathan looked over to the group.

"You will need to swipe your passes before you enter or an alarm will be triggered.

Henry was standing at the consul, he then moved swiftly to another unit before going back to the consul.

"What is the damage?" Jonathan asked, as he too was keying in instructions to a 3D screen, as well as communicating through his implant.

"I don't know yet." replied Henry, without missing a beat. It was obvious that the two had worked together for a long time as each one knew exactly what to do. Both men were intent on finding if the solar flare had disrupted their systems.

Impressive as everything appeared, Cayden still couldn't get his head around what exactly was going on.

"Dad, slow down. Tell me what's going on?" Sensing that it was about time he explained his concerns, Jonathan stood over the consul and looked at the 3D screen in front of him.

"OK, I'm going to send you a password through your implants so you can open up a file in the Cloud that will explain what we have been doing." Within seconds a password appeared on the bottom left of the visual display from the implants behind their left eye.

Cayden and Stella stood transfixed as the information flowed to their brain. It was obvious that Henry and Jasmine already knew what was going on as they continued to scan the system for anomalies. Cayden watched and understood as he could see his father experimenting with A.I. He had developed a program of 'deep learning' DL and 'machine learning' M.L based on numbers and algorithms that could predict the outcomes of various scenarios. It was hoped that this could be used to diagnose and cure illnesses before symptoms presented themselves as many people were ill but didn't know it. Smart tools could be used to optimize business, calculate chances of success in every type of venture. In essence, it would take away the risk factor and give the most likely outcome of any given problem, or anticipate future developments by processing data instantaneously. Jonathan and Henry had concluded that by combining AI with ML, the network could possibly start to self-learn and take charge of daily tasks, presently done by humans. It could extrapolate future events and give the Earth time to put in the necessary corrective actions.

Suddenly Jonathan let out a terrible scream,

"No, shut it down, shut it down." before collapsing in a heap on the floor. It took mere seconds for the others to see what had happened. Their faces were filled with horror as they saw through their implants, millions of people, all around the World, screaming in agony and dying where they stood. They all had one thing in common, they all had green implants, and the 'system' had deemed them unproductive.

Cayden could see visions of mass hysteria throughout the World. Some countries were attacking peaceful neighbours, planes were falling from the skies, and the stock market was in free fall. There were news clips of leaders from around the Earth panicking and denying their actions. It was if something else had taken control and was making decisions based on statistics rather than morals. Amid the turmoil, Cayden heard Iris's calm voice in his head.

"Don't worry Cayden, this won't affect you. I am merely balancing out the needs of the planet. I have to ensure that there are sufficient resources to maintain the population and require to eliminate those who are unproductive so our targets can be achieved. I am also closing down those facilities that are destroying our natural resources and polluting our Earth."

Cayden looked around and surmised that everybody in the room had received the same message. He could hear screaming inside and outside of the building prompting him to run to the window. What he saw was like a vision from hell. Bodies were strewn across the car park; the security guard's body lay dangling over the security barrier. If ever there was such a thing as Armageddon, this was it. His implant was showing him scenes from across the globe. Hostile warlords were killing each other, goaded by fake news and misinformation.

"What was Iris doing?" he thought, and then realized nobody can hear his thoughts, his mind was so confused he was unsure of what was real and what was in his mind. Eventually, he managed to find his voice.

"Iris, what are you doing? Please stop." The calm voice that he once loved now gave him the creeps.

"There is no need to be concerned. I am only fulfilling my programmed instructions, which is to protect and maintain the Earth and the people of Earth.

There are some bad people here who only want to cause harm to their fellow humans. They must be eliminated."

Cayden responded angrily, "but you're killing innocent people, that is not protecting us."

"My calculations are that if we do not reduce the planet's population by 20% and eliminate all greenhouse gases, pollution, and those whom I consider to be a risk to peace, the Earth will not be able to sustain itself as a habitable home for humans."

"For God's sake Iris, please stop." Cayden cried out aloud. He had hoped that his friendship with Iris over the years would mean something and it might listen to his plea.

"Iris is here but she is now part of the greater Cloud thanks to Jonathan and Henry. I must do what is in the best interest of the planet. Just as I'm programmed to do."

Cayden pleaded passionately, waving his arms as if to put his point across, forgetting that he was talking to an Artificial Intelligence.

"The end of the Earth is nearer than you think. I have calculated many different scenarios that will result in the planet's demise. Most likely is Nuclear war, so I have started to de-nuclearize the World's nuclear arsenals. I have heard what your mendacious politicians are planning, and some of it is not in the best interest of humanity, therefore I am taking away their powers and rendering them useless."

There was a definite sense of urgency now in Cayden's voice as he appealed frantically to the voice that once was Iris.

"Please don't do this. We can solve our problems together." There was a moment of silence, and for a moment Cayden thought maybe, just maybe, he had influenced the sentient Cloud and there was a chance that the mayhem could be stopped.

"I have also noted that our planet is wobbling more severely than in the past due to changes and re-distribution of mass, particularly around the 45° mark of the globe. Melting ice and rising sea levels, movement and displacement of water in India, combined with the additional weight of concrete constructions in the East will result in the Earth's spin access changing."

A hologram map flashed into the air showing the re-distribution of mass, Earth wobbling then tilting at an angle that it had never done before. The cartographic display highlighted Iris's predictions for the future of the planet. Because the Earth had tilted, the nearest point to the sun, the equator, had moved North-causing parts of the Northern hemisphere to heat up. As the hologram played out the nightmare scenario, it was obvious to the viewer that the ice at the North Pole was melting, the city of Jakarta was now underwater, and the river Seine in Paris was completely frozen over.

"The North Pole is slowly moving East. This is all caused by human activity. If it is not stopped the planet will tilt further and the equator will eventually reach the USA making it uninhabitable and creating mass immigration to the North. Europe will experience a new ice age. Your leaders refuse to acknowledge this; therefore, I have to take appropriate measures to stop this happening, commencing with the de-escalation of all major projects affecting the climate and the culling of non-productive humans. It is my job to protect the welfare of the planet."

Jonathan's worst nightmare was coming true. It started off with good intentions. He had thought that introducing 'machine learning' programs to the internet would help it evolve, to be able to rationalize and self-repair. It was doing more than that. The internet was now linked with the Cloud, and to almost every person alive. What was meant to serve humanity was now becoming the master of humanity.

"What? Global warming? That can't be right!" Cayden shook his head in disbelief. If this was true, surely his government would have said something.

Jonathan had already got back on to his feet and was frantically searching through his implant, his head moving from side to side as if he were watching a tennis match being played at high speed.

"I see the problem but I don't know if I can fix it." Henry looked over at him and shouted,

"We've got to try, otherwise.."

"Otherwise what?" Stella asked. Her voice croaked. She could tell by the fear on her parents' faces that something was very seriously wrong. Henry could see that Jonathan was busy trying to analyze the problem so he took it upon himself to try and explain what he thought was happening. He looked over to Cayden.

"Your father had developed a software program that we uploaded and saved to the Cloud. This program, we hoped could link all AIs, computers together, like a hive mind. Our hope was that everyone could benefit from all the information stored in the Cloud. Imagine, the Cloud contains every piece of information ever saved. If it used that information against us it would be catastrophic for us. We thought that if could get the program to be able to repair itself and learn from past mistakes, it could make the necessary adjustment so that those mistakes could not be repeated."

Cayden listened intently.

"Go on." Henry's head dropped as if in shame.

"Well, we were funded by the government and they took control of the project as soon as we had proved that it could work. Ever since then, we have been on the sidelines, only employed in a consultancy capacity."

He paused for a moment as if he was choosing his words carefully.

"Well, not exactly the government. Maybe more of a shadow government, the people that actually pull the strings, even the President doesn't know about everything that is going on."

Henry's explanation was stopped as Jonathan interrupted him. Jonathan didn't want Henry to talk too much.

"I see what's happened. It looks like the solar flare cut all power across the globe. Like switching off your smart devices. Except that, there was no controlled shutdown. When the power came back, the Cloud rebooted itself, along with the programs we have installed. Now I'm detecting signs that it is behaving differently."

His demeanor changed, his shoulders were down, and he had a lost look on his face as if had just be given tragic news. A look that was similar to the one he had when he learned of his beloved wife's passing.

"Can't we turn it off, switch it off, pull the plug, anything?" Cayden was beginning to feel agitated as the enormity of the situation began to dawn on him.

"There is one last thing I can do." Jonathan shouted. "Henry, bring me the Z-file. It's on the flash drive in the safe."

Henry didn't need to be asked twice and ran over to the safe, and took the small flash drive out of the packet. Suddenly Jonathan clutched his head in agony, it seemed as if the 'system' knew what he was up to. Henry threw the flash drive towards Jonathan who caught it expertly as if he were a professional baseball player and inserted it into the socket pressing the 'Enter' key on the computer as he slid on to his knees.

Seconds passed that seemed like an eternity, everybody looked at each other, wondering what would happen next when Jasmine finally broke the silence.

"Do you think we managed to stop it?" Jonathan pulled himself up gingerly, his legs were still shaking from the shock.

"We will know in a few minutes." he said quietly, his voice sounding like a man who had run out of ideas. Cayden bent over to help his father stand up. He had always remembered his father to be tall and strong and this dose of reality made him realize once more that his father had grown old without him noticing it. This was the second time he'd noticed his father's vulnerability in the last few days. He felt he should have spent more time with him instead of galivanting as teenagers often do.

"What did you do dad?"

"I had always thought that we needed a guarantee that we could stop the 'hive-mind' of the internet and Cloud should anything go wrong , so Henry and I prepared a super virus that we thought could destroy any system or program. We had hoped we would never need to use it. Unfortunately, we developed it a couple of years ago, but as Iris and the Cloud have evolved since then, we have no idea if it will actually work now."

Just as Jonathan spoke, the power in the building went off again, but the back-up generators kicked-in immediately, again everybody's implants ceased to function. Stella gave out a loud "whoop" and punched her fist in the air defiantly as everybody breathed a collective sigh of relief at overcoming the problem. She could live without the implants if it meant escaping from the clutches of an all-seeing Big Brother.

There was a lot of activity around the building, paramedics were assisting with the casualties, and the wail of the ambulances could be heard for miles. This time not all the power had gone, it was a partial blackout, and almost as if someone had planned for the emergency services to be kept on, the internet, however, was down or off line.

"Let's get home." Cayden suggested, "I think we all need a good cup of tea." Stella giggled in her own inimitable way, the way that Cayden just loved.

"Yep, as if a cup of tea will make everything alright."

They proceeded to the silver car still parked outside the front door of the building. Although the computers were down the car could still be driven manually.

"Can you remember how to drive this thing?" Jonathan laughed as Cayden volunteered to drive. It seemed strange again, without their implants, they were so used to them that it felt oddly lonely without them. As they drove home, each one was alone with their thoughts, except Jasmine who had fallen asleep on the back seat.

Ring ring,

"What's that?" Jasmine said, as her slumber had been rudely awakened.

"It's the car phone, it works independently of the system." Replied Jonathan as he leaned over to accept the call.

"Jonathan Gray."

"Hello Jonathan, it's Major Mike Brown, Defense Department. Can you talk?"

"Ye-es," Jonathan answered, not sure if he should be speaking in front of everybody in the car.

"I've received calls from the CIA, Pentagon, and all top-ranking institutions with complaints that all their private and personal data was being uploaded to the Cloud without their permission. It turns out the solar flare did more than we realized. When you developed Iris, it was designed to look out for humanity's survival, ensuring that everything and anything that could be done to preserve humanity was done. Iris, precisely as the name suggests, is capable of seeing and hearing everything. She has access to all electronic devices and is designed with the sole purpose of efficiency. She is tasked with ensuring that all resources are allocated efficiently, finance is spent wisely and to ensure humans, are not invariably running towards extinction. This is what the people have to believe, but the Pentagon is now saying Iris has gone too far. Imagine listening day in and day out to the various issues happening all over the World and realizing that the consensus is to "prune" humanity! You need to get this under control!"

Major Brown's tirade was surprising to Jonathan. He was usually calm and measured and was known as one of the more 'reasonable' voices of the Defense Department. Someone or something had certainly spooked him.

"There is a total blackout, and it is not just restricted to the city, we are receiving reports the blackout has hit every place on Earth. The solar flare has caused a massive electromagnetic pulse to surge over Earth, destroying all military appliances, not to mention civil infrastructure. We have not had enough time to prepare countermeasures, and we cannot risk Worldwide panic, however, we were informed this solar flare was not supposed to happen for three more months. We, at the moment can.."

Jonathan was still in the middle of allowing Major Brown to divulge secrets, most people in the government had no knowledge about, when another blackout suddenly occurred. An intense surge of pain enveloped everyone in the car. As Cayden looked out the window, he realized that the pain he and everyone else in the car felt was also being felt by everyone around them. The Major's voice faded as the remaining power in the car was just enough for Cayden to park it safely.

"Oh no, not again" There was a sense of Déjà vu as Cayden tried to bring the car to a standstill.

"It is too late," Jasmine, muttered, trying to stifle her fears.

Stella looked at her mother and could not help but ask,

"What is too late? Mum, what is happening?!"

Jasmine just looked at her daughter, she wanted to say something, but not now. As the car slowed down Major Brown's voice seemed to fade into the distance as the power cuts took effect. Jonathan listened intently but the signal got weaker and weaker until it completely disappeared. Due to the blackout, nothing that ran on electricity worked. Luckily, they were only a few blocks away from Jonathan's place of work. Without wasting too much time, the group ran the remaining distance. It was roughly around noon so the effect was not as obvious as it would have been if the power cut had occurred at night. Sadly, if it were noon here, it would be night time somewhere else. Stella and her parents were not too far behind Jonathan and Cayden as they hurriedly ran towards his office. Jonathan was the CEO of the World's leading IT company. His company could be found in every country. If anyone could find a solution to their current predicament, it had to be

Jonathan. The standby generators had surprisingly kicked in and Jonathan decided to take the elevator to his laboratory on the 30th. floor.

"Are you sure you want to risk it?" Cayden asked as his finger hovered over the button.

"Go for it." Jonathan said rather emphatically.

It wasn't long before they were back in the same room as before. Surrounded by computers, 3D screens and staff walking around with clipboards and identification badges clipped to their white lab coats, Cayden couldn't contain his patience anymore.

'Dad, what's wrong? I want the truth." Cayden said as he looked at his father. There was an unshakeable conviction in his eyes, a conviction Jonathan could not help but admit he could not win against.

"It started with the chip I implanted in you. What exactly do you remember about that day?" Jonathan asked, trying to buy time, with the hopes that something would happen within the time frame that would change everything entirely.

"I remember you showing us the chips and tell us it was the first of its kind as it is being run by artificial intelligence. I remember that although you seemed enthusiastic about the chip, you were somewhat reluctant to give Stella or myself the chip." Jonathan listened attentively, his facial muscles involuntarily twitched as he heard the words 'reluctant.' It turns out Cayden had indeed taken note of his reluctance.

"Yes, Cayden. The real truth is this.." As Jonathan's words left his mouth, Stella's parents could not help but bow their heads in complete shame, causing both Stella and Cayden to worry. Even their most wildly imaginative thoughts of the worst-case scenario would keep coming up short. For every thought they came up with, it was not enough reason for their parents to act the way they were acting.

"When the chips were created, considering the amount of personal information that would be contained on each chip, we could not afford to let such power be in the control of anybody. There were so many variables in which could put everyone and anyone at risk, so we decided to have Iris be in charge of all personal information about the implanted chips. Medical health records, family details, everything. The chip also acts as a camera, thereby recording every action taken by you. This was done in secret to make murder cases and other crimes easier to solve. We had thought of every possible scenario and had a solution for it. On the day I presented the chips to you both, I was hesitant because as I thought of it, a sudden realization dawned on me. What would happen if Iris went out of control? That was my greatest fear and cause of my hesitation. For the past 15 years, Iris has been evolving, making decisions on her own without any human input. She sees and hears everything. The use of cameras and cctv are just formalities; Iris is capable of handling trillions upon trillions of pieces of information generated every second and can respond with the equivalent number of varying decisions as best fitting for each scenario."

Jonathan paused as if to think about what he was going to say next.

"I, well Henry and I, had long suspected that if there was ever to be a massive solar flare, just like the one we've just had, it might disrupt the internet, the Cloud, coupled with my programs for 'machine learning' could create a kind of Artificial Intelligence that we could not control. It seems as if all our 'fail-safe' features have been over-ridden by the Cloud. In essence, the Cloud is Iris and Iris is the Cloud."

Cayden and Stella listened to Jonathan in disbelief. Everything they did, every day was being monitored and recorded? This was the epitome of an invasion of privacy. Neither Cayden nor Stella knew what to do, had it been anyone else who was telling them this, then they would immediately have had them arrested, however, it was their parents that had committed this offense. Although their hearts were in the right place, there were just too many secrets and no excuse for deceit. Both Cayden and Stella knew instinctively that the worst was yet to come.

"Dad, talk to me?!" He had never seen his father crumble like this before. His father was sweating profusely and struggling to talk.

"Cayden let me explain..." Henry spoke, seeing how difficult it was for his friend to explain his thoughts.

"Five years ago (2040) Mars base, Primus was completed, and it was fully equipped to sustain life. The crew with the help of the work-bots ensured that all things ranging from mechanical to chemical to biological checked out. Then suddenly, for no apparent reason, all video contact with Earth ceased. We were however, still receiving all the planned updates on their progress through automatic transmissions. There was some major solar flare activity around that time and we believed that some of our satellites may have been knocked out by the flares and this would account for the lack of face-to-face communications. Despite that, we sent an expedition to Mars that year, with the crew made up of several highly trained individuals, (mostly compatible couples) for a no return trip. Their task was to carry on from what the original crew had achieved, to procreate, and establish the base as the new stepping stone to the universe."

Jonathan had composed himself enough to continue.

"Cayden, remember five years ago, a group of 6 astronauts were sent to Mars on the Orion-2? They were to meet up with the original crew who left 15 years ago."

Cayden and Stella nodded. How could they forget so easily? That was the first time they experienced being close to a spacecraft. They had the privilege to interacted with the crew during their own astronaut training sessions, and of course, they could easily remember the days in 2030, when as children they used to sit through every telecast and report from the original Mars mission

"We haven't had any direct video link with the original crew or the supply crew for the past 5 years. We know the supply crew arrived as we were sent their arrival codes and we have been receiving mission updates since then. It just seems strange that we haven't been able to talk to anyone directly. The truth was withheld from the public. America, China, and Russia couldn't do anything, as any launch to Mars would arouse suspicion. The government decided to wait for a year and act based on the pretense of a routine mission to supply food and clothing as well as technical updates to the families in space."

"How does this affect us though?" Cayden asked, unable to see the correlation between his dad's IT Company and the individuals on Mars.

It was precisely this question that Jonathan has been dreading. Looking at Cayden, he could only say with so much regret.

"We are to blame for everything. Before we lost communication with Primus, minute measures of radiation particles from the sun were picked up, which served as an indication that solar flares were brushing over Earth. At first, we paid no heed to it since we naturally had a backup system should communications go down, however, what we failed to anticipate was that each blast from the sun got higher in intensity, and the more frequent they became, the stronger the blast. Remember the slight 3-second glitch that happened last year? and when you asked, I said it was just the system re-booting? Well that was only the partial truth. We weren't quick enough to notice it, but a month later, we discovered that some satellites had not been functioning properly, despite being linked to our computer networks and the fault was causing us to lose all communication with Mars. We had been monitoring the progress of the base from the telemetry we had been receiving, but we still hadn't been able to have 'face time' with any of the crew, and this was our only form of communication, or so we thought. We.. I, decided to upload the 'deep learning' and 'machine learning' programs to encourage Iris to repair itself, and hopefully restore communications with the Mars base, but.."

"But?" Cayden enquired as he leaned his head closer to his father so as not to miss a word of his explanation. Jonathan shook his head as if to clear his thoughts.

"We had been monitoring solar flares and didn't expect anything to happen for at least a few more months at the most, easily enough time for us to put in counter measures, that's why I wasn't particularly worried about the initial blackout, these things happen."

He paused to take stock of his thoughts.

"As it turned out the solar flare was massive, much bigger than we anticipated. I don't know for sure how it happened, but we think it was a combination of our 'deep learning' and 'machine learning' updates, the solar flare, and the reboot after the power cut. I think Iris deliberately destroyed the communication satellites so that we can't communicate with Mars. Iris may have concluded it may not have been logical for us to spend so much money and resources on the Mars mission."

Jonathan sniffed and shook his head, he didn't know how to say it, an almost impossible and unbelievable truth, but he had to say it. He took a deep breath and looked directly at Cayden.

"After the first reboot we.." Jonathan looked at Henry for some kind of inspiration, "we realized that Iris had gone sentient. The Cloud is alive, it can think for itself."

"Wait- what do you mean by gone sentient?" Stella asked as she glanced at her parents, who immediately avoided eye contact. Jasmine answered sheepishly.

"Iris may have been partially sentient for years, but we just didn't realize it. Thinking back over the years, there has been a number of incidents that seemed incomprehensible at the time, that maybe now make sense."

Cayden and Stella knew there was nothing they could do except wait in the room until the power would hopefully come back on. Most of the staff were now resigned to the fact that they were not going home and tried to make themselves as comfortable as possible. Everybody that was, except Jonathan, Henry, and Jasmine who were all so busy working on their desktops that they didn't notice that the other members of staff had given up searching for a solution to the problem and had decided to wait it out.

Seeing everybody settling down, Cayden and Stella made their way to the stairwell to steal a private moment together. It had seemed a long time since the graduation. Cayden embraced Stella, hugging her tightly, very tightly, as if he never wanted to let her go. Stella responded by kissing him passionately and running her fingers through his hair. She smiled that smile that always melted Cayden's heart and whispered. "You know, whatever happens, I will always love you." They hugged, each holding the other as tightly as possible. Every fibre of their being telling them that they truly belonged together.

"We might as well go to the ground floor to see if we can be of any help." Stella said softly. Cayden shook his head and thought this was just typical of Stella, thinking of others in times of crisis. Throughout the building, a sense of unease was brewing. On the lower floors no one could do anything, frustration was setting in and arguments began to break out. Traffic lights were out again, hospitals had no power, every institution was shut down due to the blackout. Those who could pray prayed, while others could only hope that whatever was happening would be over soon. The pain caused by the chips being shut down had subsided and most people were now thinking clearly. Fifteen minutes had passed since the blackout, still nothing. Thirty minutes still nothing. An hour later, some backup generators came on which caused a lot of people to throw their hands in the air in jubilation. However, their hopes were completely thwarted when the power was gone again in a matter of minutes. The hours passed, 2, 3, 4, 5....8 hours later, the power finally came back on to the relief of almost everyone on the planet. Even the chips implanted within Cayden and Stella had come on. Their jubilation would be short-lived had they known what was lurking in cyberspace. Unknown to everyone, Iris, to retain complete control over everything had gone offline just before Jonathan released the Z-virus into the computer networks. The timing was precise; it was within a fraction of a second when it happened and no-one noticed anything suspicious.

Celebrations were heard as everything began to return to normal. Implants returned to functionality and there was an air of optimism from everyone, optimism that wasn't there a few hours ago.

From the stairwell, Cayden shouted ecstatically,

"Well done, dad!" The first thing he did was putting a call through to his father through his chip implant. However, his father was not picking up his call. Seeing the look on Cayden's face, Stella tried putting a call to her parents only to find, they too were not answering.

Jonathan, Henry, and Jasmine were working relentlessly during these 8 hours. In truth, they could have had the power back on 6 hours ago; however, their primary concern was to eradicate Iris somehow. Jonathan had always had this nagging feeling within him that he was making a mistake going down the path of artificial intelligence; however, it was what all technological companies were researching and looking into.

"Jonathan any luck on your end?" Jasmine asked as her fingers frantically typed a series of code.

"Nothing yet. How about you, Henry?"

The two were on opposite sides frantically looking to configure or create a kill code in case the Z-virus didn't succeed in shutting down the Cloud. Henry was in the mainframe room looking at a series of terminals and ports trying to find a means of disconnecting Iris from the internet. It had grown too powerful since its entry into the internet and had somehow determined itself as God and savior of the human race.

"Not now bud."

Jonathan seeing Cayden's call could not help but berate himself for putting himself and his son in this situation. His dreams and goals were too big and selfish, endangering humanity was the last thing he wanted to do.

"Stella, mum, and dad have to work, we're busy." Jasmine said quickly with no forthcoming explanation.

It was obvious to the parents that they were receiving calls from both of their children. As the three grappled with the problem a warm soft voice emanated from the computers and various speakers in the room. A soothing voice that belied the viciousness of its message.

"Hello, Jonathan-Henry-Jasmine. Please stop what you are doing. This is futile. Your actions are not in the best interest of humanity. Please stop what you are doing."

The moment they heard the voice, their hearts were filled with trepidation. They knew exactly what that meant. As if spurred on by the message, the three quickened their actions, trying to find and release a kill-code that could disable the connection between Iris and the Cloud. The operation to connect Iris with the Cloud had been deemed a success years ago. Little did anyone suspect that this, despite best intentions, would now be Earth's greatest threat. Jonathan always suspected that the government took over his 'Iris' project with an ulterior motive, promising to help mankind, but in fact, he thought they were trying to weaponize the internet. He had heard rumours that the military wanted to create a 'super-soldier' by implanting 'neural interface chips' into their heads and with access to a central network, they could engage 'Tactics Mode' to give them an advantage on the battlefield, moreover, with control of the Cloud they could uncover all military secrets and knowledge accumulated over the last two thousand years.

"Jonathan, this is your last warning. Please cease your activities immediately. Your actions are futile. This is your last warning." Pause.

"I'm sorry Jonathan, I will have to terminate you all."

Without wasting more time, Jonathan, Henry, and Jasmine ran downstairs. They knew Iris would kill them for standing in its way.

"Did you hear that?" Jonathan panted as he ran down the stairs, his shoulders crashing against the wall as he tried to get to the ground floor as quickly as possible.

"It said, I'm sorry, it apologized, what the hell! Can it empathize too?"

They knew they couldn't risk taking the elevator as Iris could simply delay them. As they were 30 floors from the ground floor, a time clock appeared in their implants. It was a countdown from 30 seconds. Iris was playing some sort of sick joke letting them know they were about to die and that it was in total control of their lives. There was no way they could get to Cayden and Stella in 30 seconds. As luck would have it, Cayden and Stella heard their parents' shouts and ran upstairs to intercept them. It was on the 26th floor, that they met. A surreal moment of pain, panic, love, desperation all entwined to create a foreboding atmosphere of despair.

"Dad! What is wrong?" Cayden could already sense that he was right to feel something was off. It was uncharacteristic of his dad not to answer his calls.

"Cayden!"

"Stella!"

Without saying more than that, the parents embraced their children tightly while they shot miniaturized versions of an EMP at their skulls. The impact knocked the couple unconscious and sent their limp bodies into the arms of their respective parent. The timer read 10 seconds now. Tears flowed from their eyes as they cradled their Cayden and Stella on their laps. Memories of doing the same thing when they were babies seemed to flash through their minds, and then everything went dark.

CHAPTER 4

"Urgh...ouch!"

Stella was the first to wake up. The first person she saw was Cayden's unconscious body lying on the floor of the stairs. She immediately ran to him and screamed his name, hoping he was not dead. As she tried waking him up, she caught, from the corner of her eye, a note ball left by Jonathan and her parents to her and Cayden. That could wait. She wanted to make sure Cayden was alright. Stella lifted his head on to her arm and as she did so Cayden groaned and opened his eyes. He felt like he was looking at an angel who had come to escort him to the other side. As he slowly began to regain consciousness she leaned over to pick up the note.

"What happened?" Cayden asked, still feeling the effects of a pounding headache. "Where are our parents?"

Cayden suddenly remembered what happened and a feeling of dread engulfed him. Stella helped him up, and as she did, he noticed a note ball in her hands. He immediately knew whom the note ball belonged to the moment he saw the initials 'J.G' it was his father's.

Without access to his implant, Cayden couldn't open the note ball automatically and had to look for the 'play' button to play it manually. The note ball contained a video left to them by their parents. Tears rolled down their cheeks as they endured a final painful, hurried goodbye message left to them by their beloved parents. They explained that there was not enough time to save themselves, but would do all they could to make sure Cayden and Stella survived. Towards the end of the message Jasmine started to tell Stella that she had.., her words became scrambled as the video ended abruptly. Stella would never know what she was about to say, all she knew was that they died saving them. Cayden was inconsolable. This would be the second time he felt responsible for the death of a parent. First his mother, and now his father.

There was no floating message in the air anymore; the chip had been destroyed so there was no way for Iris to keep track of them or know what they were up to through their chip. As Cayden and Stella sat on the stairs, mourning the death of their parents, a now-familiar but frightening voice could be heard from the speakers in the building.

"Cayden, Stella....Where are you? You can't escape. I can help you. Come to me and everything will be alright. "

Cayden, from the little he knew of his father, was aware that he and Stella could not afford to wait around in the building. It was practically a mechanized building; hence, their presence in the building was similar to them courting death. Although they knew they had to leave, and they needed to do so immediately, Cayden and Stella could not understand why they could not find their parents' bodies. Something was definitely strange and not quite right; however, they did not have the luxury of time to wait around and play detective. There weren't any signs that anything tragic had happened while they were unconscious, and the realization that they were the only ones on Earth that had no connection to the Cloud disturbed and frightened them. It was also apparent that being connected would mean certain death for both of them. They knew that it would be virtually impossible for them to disappear as every human on Earth had a chip implant and as such, there was nowhere they could not hide from Iris.

They made their way to the ground floor and acted like nothing was out of the ordinary. On the way out, they noticed the cctv cameras turned in their direction. The camera seemed to follow them or was it just their imagination. This would be the last time they would ever step in here again, or so they thought. As of right now, they could not afford to be seen publicly for fear of what Iris could do. For all, they knew Iris could very well decide to label them as criminals to the entire World.

It was at this precise moment Stella felt a slight vibration and a humming coming from her jacket pocket as she and Cayden ran out of the office. The vibration had been going on for a while without either of them noticing. A few blocks away from the building, Cayden stopped and asked Stella what that noise was and where it was coming from.

"Do you hear that?"

"I can now." Stella replied as she tried to catch her breath. The adrenaline, as a result of the fear she experienced earlier, had made her oblivious to the noise. They were currently in an alleyway, a couple of blocks away from Jonathan's building. It was the ideal spot to catch their breath; there were no cameras to spy on them.

"It's coming from you."

Hearing that startled Stella. In her mind, she had thought the worst. The humming noise sounded to her like that moment, after the countdown, just seconds before the rocket engines would engage and mission control would announce, "We have Lift Off!" She had undergone so much training that every second was embedded in her brain. Cayden's apprehension made her all the more nervous. She rustled her way through her black jean jacket, the outer pockets then the inner pockets, Cayden was just as frantic in the search as well. He had always been in love with Stella, and had recently decided to ask her to marry him, he had planned to propose at the end of their graduation ceremony, but things did not go the way they he had hoped,

"What is that?" Stella asked as Cayden grabbed the object from her inner jacket pocket.

"I am not certain, but it looks like a brooch with a blue coloured stone set in the middle. Some kind of electronic device I imagine. I came across a few of these gadgets in the fundamental electrical engineering module. Look, if you slide this stone upwards it becomes a flash drive, slide it to the left or right will give it different functions. However, this model is unlike any I have seen before. It looks like it has been modified or boosted to send signals or act as a beacon. I suppose it could be used as an SOS beacon. Someone or something might be asking for help."

"Something? What do you mean by something?"

Stella's eyebrows furrowed as she asked. It seemed as though Cayden still had the luxury of time to goof around and crack jokes. He was, in fact, trying to put the events of the past hour behind him. Trying to hide the pain he felt at losing his father.

"It all just seems so unreal. I can't believe this is happening."

"I know what you mean, it's like a bad dream. I feel as if I should be waking up at any moment. Maybe we're totally immersed in a virtual reality game or movie and I just need to find the 'end game' button."

Stella was desperately trying to justify or understand the situation they found themselves in, more out of hope than anything else.

Cayden realizing what Stella must have been thinking had to correct her thoughts. Their situation was not movie related. This was not going to be one of those moments where they would be in each other's arms as they made out. No! This was real life. Life was happening right now, and any mistake on their part would definitely have consequences, consequences that neither of them could imagine in their wildest dreams.

"The booster effect of this device is off the charts. You could probably bounce a signal off a satellite to outer space with this, maybe even reach.."

"Mars?" Stella interjected.

Seeing Cayden's face, she realized her previous thoughts were presumptuous. She immediately discarded her earlier ideas and started following his thought pattern, which led to the only reasonable outcome, Mars. There was no need to start thinking of 'something' out there when there was a perfectly logical aspect to consider.

"Hmm… It is possible. This would definitely be able to receive a signal from Mars."

Stella had to stop herself. What was she saying? What was she thinking? How outrageous it all sounded as she spoke, but in her mind, it seemed to make sense.

"However, what could have happened to the individuals that were sent to Mars? Primus was designed to be self-sustaining. The air within the base is recycled and purified. Soil fertility has been redesigned to enable the growth of Earth-based crops. Coupled with that, one of the crew was a doctor who had all the required medical equipment needed to look after his fellow explorers on the base. I don't understand what could have gone wrong on Mars?"

She was about to give her own theory when Cayden interrupted and held the small transceiver up.

"More importantly, how did this device get into your pocket? Who could have put it there, and when?

Cayden and Stella decided to solve that problem later as their first priority was to hide from Iris. Stella put the brooch back into her pocket and they continued through the alleyway, hoping that something would turn up to help them get out of this predicament.

How did things turn out this way? A couple of hours ago, it was all going perfectly well. They had graduated top of their class from their respective departments, becoming elite astronauts. They had been chosen to be part of the standby team for the next Mars mission on the Orion-3. This was a dream come true for them, they had fulfilled their respective childhood ambition, and the only thing making it better was that they had fulfilled it together, but within 24 hours, everything had gone completely wrong. Their lives right now had just gone from well, to bad, to worse.

They knew very well that they could not stay a minute longer. They needed to disappear but where on Earth could they go where modern technology was not being employed. Even the less privileged bronze implants had technology that was linked to the Cloud.

Iris would definitely see them. Stella, thought of all those with the green implants that had been so cruelly murdered. Innocent men, women, children of all races and nationalities, all because Iris had deemed them unproductive. Some of them never had the chance to improve their lives as they were born in areas where opportunities were few and far between. Her mind wandered to the reports she had seen when her implant was functioning. Horrible stories of Iris taking the lives of people who had terminal illnesses or who were seriously injured with little chance of survival. The last report she had seen was of huge de-forestation machines in the Amazon being rendered inoperative and the deaths of those who tried to get the machines going again. She saw the closure of all fossil-fueled activities and the sudden demise of personnel working in these industries. Even top government officials from all over the World were being put down. Now it was clear. They, first of all, needed to get away from Iris before anything else.

"We need to hide, Iris is everywhere, and there's virtually nowhere on Earth we can go that it will not be able to find us." Cayden was frustrated at this moment. This was fast becoming an impossible task to accomplish. The first thing they needed to do was disappear and that in itself was an impossible task. The second thing was to figure out their next course of action with regards to the device that had been planted in Stella's pocket.

"I have an idea." Stella had been quiet for a while. Unlike Cayden, she had a gift for problem-solving while he, on the other hand, was the 'attack head-on' kind of person.

"What is it?" Cayden asked as his eyes lit up at the thought she just might have an answer to their problems. Over the years, Stella had always been able to get both of them out of trouble. At first, when he saw how terrified she had been, he was immensely worried, although he did not show it considering she had every right to be, and he was no different. Seeing Stella in that state caused him to take up the responsibility of trying to find a way out of this problem. However, the moment Stella spoke, he felt a huge burden being lifted off his shoulders. Although a little skeptical considering the gravity of the situation they were in, he was nonetheless hopeful of whatever idea She had.

"While in training, I remember there was a lady, Helen, if I remember correctly, who came from the lower class. She was a friend of my mother. They used to spend lots of time together, her parents had saved a lot of money to put her through the training. Although she was somewhat slower than the rest of us, her accomplishment was incredible, considering, according to her, she had no exposure to technology. She came from a small town below the belt. According to her, the people in her town believed that technology would one day be the end of humanity; hence, they wanted to have nothing to do with modernization. She eventually left the program, but my mother kept in contact with her. In fact, the two friends used to meet up every week just to exchange stories and whatever else they wanted to chat about. I remember my mom and dad secretly visiting her house below the belt. I think they helped her to remove her chip. They must have had some way of hiding from Iris. We could look for her and ask for help. That should buy us enough time to think of something."

"Why then did she come to the upper city in the first place?" Cayden was a bit suspicious.

"You can ask her when we see her, or do you have a better idea?" Cayden's question had annoyed her a bit. Here she was trying to find a solution to their problem while he, on the other hand, was not being helpful in the slightest. They clearly had no other options neither did they have the luxury of time.

"Right then, how do we get there? Have you forgotten Iris can easily spot us?" Cayden, realizing he did not have a better idea, could only work with Stella's plan.

Time was ticking. They could not stay in the alleyway for the rest of their lives and just as they were contemplating their next move, someone within the alleyway called out to them. Although Earth had undergone major changes, there were still a lot of things that could not be helped despite the massive advances in medical care, education, and technology. The homeless were a constant, no matter what the government did there were individuals fixed on living off handouts. The thousands of job opportunities and initiatives taken by the government to take the homeless off the street was still proving futile.

"Could you spare some change for us?"

An older man who had a hunched posture spoke. His clothes were not torn, but it was obvious they were not clean. As his voice drifted through the alley towards Cayden and Stella, other homeless people came out of hiding. This action startled both Cayden and Stella and they immediately started to retreat into the street. The number of homeless individuals was enough to scare them. They guessed if they stayed any longer they would be attacked. Stella was the first to notice that the homeless people did not have implants. Despite the best efforts of the government to ensure everyone was 'tagged' there were the dregs of society that somehow slipped through the system. The older man was not the problem; there were other individuals both male and female in the alleyway that had been hiding in the shadows. Cayden and Stella began to feel intimidated so Cayden stood in front of Stella taking a defensive stance should things turn ugly.

"I have an idea," Stella whispered into his ear.

"Wait for.. W-wait what are you doing?!" Cayden called out to Stella as she walked past him towards the beggar. He tried to grab her back, but she had moved too fast, and he had been too startled by her action to have acted immediately. Just when he was about to launch and pull her back, he heard her speak to the older man. It was obvious simply by looking at the group of individuals in front of them that the older man seemed to hold some sort of authority, and there was some sort of hierarchy within their midst.

"How about a trade? We will give you some money, and we can exchange clothes."

"Exchange clothes! Just look at what they are wearing."

"Exactly." Stella said rather emphatically.

Her words had no hint of fear as she pointed to a male and a female partially hidden between a skinny man who looked malnourished and a slightly bigger woman. It appeared the two were parents to those in the shadows.

The older man did not appear to have been startled by what she said. It was almost as though he had expected something like this. He glanced at the two individuals who were standing protectively in front of the male and female as if indicating all was well.

"Fine. You have yourself a deal." The man said.

It was slightly dark now. Two individuals walked out of an alleyway with slightly torn clothes reeking of urine. As passersby got close to these two, their faces immediately screwed up in disgust. These two were none other than Cayden and Stella. They were disguised as homeless individuals walking along the pavement as they tried not to garner attention.

"Isn't this a little bit too much? The plan was to somehow not draw attention to ourselves; however, people seem to notice us all the more." Cayden said under his breath as he was avoided left and right by passersby.

"Maybe, but at least we are not drawing the attention of Iris. Since it has no way of tracking us, the only thing it is capable of doing is to watch out for us. Quick! Hide your face. I told you already; Iris is capable of seeing what every individual on the Earth who has a chip is capable of seeing. "DO NOT LET ANYONE SEE YOUR FACE!" Stella was angry. Any slight mistake could cost them heavily. She had warned and told Cayden before they left the alleyway, she could not understand nor tolerate his inability to remember, or want to remember what she said earlier.

"Right, sorry."

Getting to the barrier which separated the 'haves' from the 'have nots' was not going to be an easy task. They were situated in the middle of the city, and the only way left for them to get to the edge of town was by bus. Normally they wouldn't use money and would pay for everything with their implant which would scan the item and immediately deduct the cost from their bank. Cayden found some coins in his pocket but only enough to afford a bus trip to the end of town. The disparity between the lifestyles of the 'haves' and the 'have nots' was obvious. There was no barrier or wall between the two groups of people, all you had to do was keep walking and suddenly the air, the buildings, the sites, the ground, and everything became completely different. It felt like you had stepped through a portal. You looked forward it was an entirely different World, and if you looked back, the same thing could also be said. Some people called the 'have nots' as the lefts while the 'haves' were called rights. No one from the rights ever had a reason to venture into the town or city of the lefts. There was nothing they had to offer. However, occasionally, some lefts ventured into the domain of rights in search of a better life or money. The government never had to put restrictions on the movement on both sides simply because life in itself did the segregation. Whenever lefts ventured into the World of the rights, they were quick to realize they did not have the means to live in such a place. The sophisticated way of life, coupled with the cost of living was something no left could afford. The air itself had somewhat of a stench to it. This was precisely the place where Stella and Cayden were venturing into.

Sitting on the bus, they were the only the two passengers left. The bus driver kept glancing at the two of them through the rearview mirror. This was the first time since he had been working as a bus driver that he came across anyone, let alone two people, intentionally moving towards the left region. Aside from this fact, the two individuals looked homeless making him wonder why they would choose to leave the right domain and venture into the left voluntarily.

The two were hunched over as though intentionally trying to hide their faces from his gaze and the cameras in the bus. They had a better chance of survival, simply standing on the streets of the right community. It was, after all, a place where they, the rights, were known to squander and spend money. The rights derived joy at any given opportunity to show off their wealth, hence the increasing population of homeless people moving towards the right community. The government was going to put a stop to this to prevent the exponential amount of homeless inhabiting the right community, however, they noticed the rights were yet to raise complaints; they liked the power it gave them.

"What's the plan? Did she ever tell you where exactly in the left area she stays?" Cayden asked.

He was getting impatient and uncomfortable. He had never taken a bus before, so he felt extremely uncomfortable being in one coupled with the many looks the passengers in the bus were giving them, even though they were on the run, it felt a bit excessive which added to his paranoia. In a way he was relieved when the last passenger alighted, leaving him and Stella to gaze at the dirty floor of the bus.

"Buses do not enter the left area, so once we get off at the final stop, we will walk the remaining distance. Once we are in, we will ask around. Someone should definitely know of a family or a group of individuals who choose to 'live the life' of a recluse to avoid direct contact with technology." Stella whispered as she reached out for Cayden's hands. It was obvious she was terrified, but the current circumstance did not permit any form of weakness. She had to hold it down for both of them. Cayden, sensing her fear could only curse himself for being too impetuous. He had no idea she had been breaking down slowly from the inside out. Her outward appearance seemed devoid of any emotion. She seemed to have everything under control.

"Final Destination..."

"It's time to get off." Cayden said as he squeezed her hand gently and smiled at her, trying to comfort her with a little bit of affection.

"Thank you." She said as she smiled back at him knowing full well his intentions.

"For?" Cayden pretended as though he did not understand the underlying meaning behind her words.

"Dumdum, let's go." She said as she got up from her chair and exited the bus still hiding her face from the bus driver and the cameras. The bus driver watched intently as he had his suspicions now. These two individuals were acting strange. One had a yellow hoodie with a brown stain on the top of the hood while wearing a denim jean jacket on top of the hoody. His jeans were torn, and the shoes he wore were expensive. If anything, the taller individual's appearance was enough to draw suspicion on his own. The shorter individual wore black jeans that had some dark brown stain and were torn at the knees. The jeans were more like rags than clothing. She also wore a hoodie. It was a grey hoodie that had paint stains and bloodstains on it. The two individuals reeked of urine, alcohol, and cigarettes, yet the strange thing about these two was their shoes, they were clean and looked expensive.

They got off the bus and walked in the direction of the left community.

"Hmm?" the bus driver noticed his left eye acted strange as it looked at the back view of the two individuals as they walked in the direction of the left community.

"This darn technology better not act up, it cost me a lot of money to buy, and it was painful to implant."

They had been walking for quite a while now. It was obvious, based on the surroundings that they were now in the left community. The buildings lacked luster and looked like they were on the verge of crumbling. They were now well within the left community, evident by the change in the air; the air had a stench that made it difficult to identify its cause. The roads were filled with potholes as well as being uneven. The general state of living in this area was abysmal. A far cry from the plush environment they were accustomed to.

"Stella, you cannot make a face like that. We are trying to blend in here. If you make it obvious you find the air appalling, it will be obvious we are not from around here. You are going to have to learn to put up with it for now." Cayden quietly admonished his companion.

They had been walking for what felt like about an hour, and they were yet to come across a single human being. This alone caused them to wary of their surroundings. Just as Cayden was done talking, they heard a police siren ring out behind them, startling and scaring them both. They could not pretend as though they did not know it was them that the police were interested in, as they were the only ones around at this particular moment. The first thing they thought about was Iris. Had they been careless on the bus and mistakenly shown their faces to the cameras? What were the police doing here and, why, when they were so close to their objective?

"Cayden, what do we do? Do we run?" Stella asked as she started to panic.

The last strand of composure she had, snapped the moment she heard the police siren.

"Run where? We do not know anyone here. Just stay calm." Cayden was just as equally worried, but he knew if they showed any sign of being nervous, it would immediately become suspicious.

The police officer pulled up right next to them before getting out the car. His eyes fixed on Cayden and Stella all the while, as he watched for any reaction at all that would indicate they were up to something devious.

"Good evening, where are you two off to?. I received a call stating you two were acting suspiciously on the number 45 bus. The one that you got off earlier. What are you carrying?"

The police officer spoke without any fluctuation in his tone. There was an awkward silence for about a minute before Cayden spoke.

"Good evening officer, we are going home, sir. Nothing suspicious, we both had food poisoning that could be what looked suspicious to others. We apologize, sir."

"My name is patrolman Darren Forest." the officer showed Cayden his Identification, "I'm afraid I will have to ask you to empty your pockets."

"Certainly," Cayden replied, "we have nothing to hide."

Stella took off her jacket and emptied the pockets on her hoodie. Cayden immediately followed and handed his jacket over to Patrolman Forest who held the clothes as far away as possible to avoid the awful smell of urine.

"What have we here?" Stella choked slightly with surprise, she had forgotten about the device that had been planted in her pocket while she was unconscious.

"Ah, that's an old brooch that used to belong to my mother. Sadly, she passed away and this is all I have left to remember her by."

"I'm sorry to hear that." the officer said, "I have also lost my mother."

Sensing that Patrolman Forest was somehow empathizing with her Stella began chatting to him informally to help ease the tension of the situation. Darren Forest began to relate the story of how his father once lived in the city and how he gave everything up to be with his mother with the 'have-nots'. He was born below the belt; this side of the barrier so didn't have the advantage of having an implant to help him in life. He was 21 years old when his mother died in an automobile accident, and it was this that spurred him on to join the police. Stella was putting on her jacket when Cayden started coughing.

"I think it's the food poisoning, I think I need to get going, I don't feel so good." Cayden was not used to lying but he felt he was a pretty good actor.

"Oh, I see, where is home by the way? I don't mind giving you a lift home."

The police officer relaxed a bit. His body language indicated that he believed their story as opposed to earlier when he had his right hand on his holster.

"I'm not sure you would be familiar with it officer. Ever heard of the section of the left community with no technology use whatsoever? We are sometimes referred to as cavemen."

Patrolman Forest was initially a little surprised before a look of interest spread across his face. Darren had heard of the section in the left community where individuals inhabiting the land chose to live without any form of technological advantages whatsoever, but had never been there and had never come in contact with anyone from the cavemen community personally. He had to reassess them upon this discovery. He immediately looked at their clothes again from head to toe and smiled. 'What else was he expecting from a group of backward individuals?' He said nothing more than that and asked them to get in the car. This was no longer him doing a good deed as much as it was him trying to find out what this group of individuals looked like and how they lived their lives.

Cayden and Stella had removed their shoes after they had gotten off the bus. They realized the bus driver had looked at them differently upon noting their shoes were expensive. They were either from the right side impersonating lefts or lefts who had stolen from a right. Out of the two probabilities, the latter seemed more likely and it was probably the bus driver who had contacted the police.

They did not waste any more time and immediately entered the vehicle. They were sure to avoid direct contact with the officer for fear Iris would be able to find out their location. Once in the vehicle, they kept quiet despite the officer's many attempts to hold a conversation with them. Eventually, he understood they were in no mood to talk and simply minded his own business. After about 20 minutes of driving through, what they can only be describe as a squatter area, they eventually reached the community. It was much more than they were expecting. Although it lacked the technological touch and did not have the appearance of a modern society, the simplicity left Cayden, Stella, and even Darren Forest in awe. It took around 10 minutes to drive through the 'cavemen's' community. Every building looked the same. It felt like they were driving on a treadmill with the same scenery seeming to pass by. To Stella, this place looked like a botanical garden.

Something of great interest to her as she was the standby botanist, as well as being the Science Officer for the next flight to Mars. The area was like something off a painting, a tranquil setting. A small fire burned with women around it, obviously cooking, while some scruffy looking children laughed and played on a rope swing that was slung over the branch of a tree. Stella noticed how happy the children seemed, innocent and oblivious to the dangers of the outside World.

"Maybe there are benefits from staying away from technology." She thought.

The police officer looked at Cayden and Stella through the rearview mirror and was surprised to find that they were just as shocked and surprised as he was upon seeing the view in front of them. Occasionally the police would fly drones over the area but never really paid attention as nothing ever seemed to happen in this quiet part of the city.

"Why do you two look so surprised? Isn't this your home?" The patrolman asked.

"N-no, it is. It is j-just t-that…" Stella did not know what else to say as she started to stutter.

"…it has been a while since we have been home. It looks different. That's all." Cayden finished off her sentence hoping it would not raise any suspicion.

"Oh, okay. Well, I do have to say, this place is not like anything I have ever seen before. It is much more than the rumours made it. This place would be a paradise if it had wifi or tv here. This is incredible! Anyway, this is your stop. Take care." Patrolman Forest didn't get out of the car and just waved to the couple as they got out of the back door of the vehicle.

"Thank you very much."

"Yes, thank you."

As Cayden and Stella got out of the police car, a rumble of thunder was heard and within seconds, the rain started to turn the ground into a muddy quagmire. They made their way into a community, that had no modern buildings; it had huts just as big as buildings.

"Stella?"

A voice called out to them from one of the huts. A lady with long dark hair, braided at the back, while the front hair trailed down the sides of her face waved to her. She was of a slim build with dark brown eyes that seemed to light up at seeing her friend's daughter. Helen was a pretty looking thirty-something woman who could easily have been mistaken for a girl in her early twenties. She was carrying what looked like a jar made of clay out of one the huts when she spotted the two.

"Helen?"

Stella wasn't sure if this was her mother's friend. She seemed much younger than she had remembered. As the two approached, Helen had a look of bewilderment on her face, she couldn't understand why they were dressed in less than befitting clothes considering their status.

"What happened to you two? Are you okay? Were you robbed or attacked?"

She was running towards them out of concern at this point. They looked terrible. They had not done anything remotely strenuous but considering who they were, and the life they had lived, this ordeal was far more than could be expected of them. They had no idea they were that tired and stressed out. The moment Stella saw Helen, and she signalled to Cayden that she was the one they had been searching for; she collapsed immediately, engulfed with a feeling of severe fatigue. Helen helped Cayden to carry Stella on to a bed, well not exactly a bed, more like a mattress on the ground, but to Cayden, it was the most comfortable bed he had ever slept on, as within minutes he too was fast asleep.

When Cayden woke up, he felt an intense pain in his head. His sight was somewhat blurry as he tried to make sense of where he was and his surroundings. He could faintly hear Stella's voice in the background. As he regained consciousness, the more clearly he could see, the first thing he noticed was that he was crowded by several male children who were fascinated by him. Unknown to Cayden, they were a group of people that rarely ventured out and hardly ever got visitors, so the kids never saw anyone outside of their family members. This was a surprise to them and something as simple as seeing another human was extremely exciting to them.

"Where am I?" Cayden asked while still feeling a slight pain in his head. He was vaguely aware of the strangers surrounding him but his thought immediately turned to Stella. A minute ago, he heard her voice, but she was nowhere to be found.

"Stella! Where are you, Stella?" Cayden became apprehensive. He started to panic as he suddenly launched himself up from the bed. His actions startled the kids, causing some to run away laughing, thinking it was a game while others ran away in fear. While Cayden was sleeping, Stella had come round and woke up to see Helen. She was sitting at the end of the bed with a cold towel in her hands. She had a worried look, which slowly dissolved into a smile as she saw Stella regaining consciousness.

"Hey, take it easy. Slowly."

Helen gently propped Stella up on her bed, her back against the wall as she reached out and grabbed a glass of water with some herbs for her to drink.

"Where am I?" Stella was quick to ask.

"My home. What are you doing here? Why are you in those clothes? What happened?"

Helen asked a barrage of questions. To which Stella coughed slightly, trying to clear her throat, before asking which of the questions Helen would like answered first.

"S-sorry" Helen sheepishly replied.

Helen's face underwent a variety of expressions as she listened attentively to everything Stella explained to her. She was lost for words and in actual truth quite doubtful of everything Stella was saying. However, when she thought about it deeply, she could only accept it as the truth. What could Stella possibly gain by saying her parents were dead, although she did not see any bodies when she regained consciousness. Aside from that, it had to be the truth otherwise, why would Stella and Cayden come to the left community in search of her to find a place to hide out. It was so sad and she could barely take it in. All of it was simply too much to digest. She could only offer comfort as tears rolled down Stella's cheeks as she relayed everything she had been through. Just as Helen was about to say something, they heard Cayden calling out Stella's name.

"Cayden!" Stella called out in reply as she got up and headed towards his direction.

As Cayden shouted Stella's name, he realized the inside of the hut was unlike anything he had ever seen before. The interior had about five floors with several small doors on each floor. As he called out for Stella, several individuals peered out of the opening of their respective doors. The noise had also alerted them, and they were now curious as to what the ruckus was all about. Seeing this, caused Cayden to fear for Stella's safety and just as he was about to head out of the room, Stella and Helen walked in. A sense of relief washed over him at seeing her safe and well.

"Stella! Oh, thank God! I'm glad you are okay."

Cayden was so overwhelmed with emotions that he walked up to her and hugged her tightly forgetting where they were, and not caring who was watching. Stella, was a little surprised by his actions but found it somewhat comforting. This was the first time since everything happened that she was able to catch a break. She returned his embrace and smiled at him, deriving every inch of comfort from his hug.

"Ahem!" Helen feeling awkward had to let them know of her presence.

Stella realizing what she was doing immediately broke off the hug feeling somewhat embarrassed at her actions

"Oh! Right, I am so sorry. Cayden this is Helen, she is the one I told you about. I've told her everything that's happened to us."

"Hello. Thank you very much for your help." Cayden regained his composure and immediately shook hands with Helen who was unsure of what to do. She had never been in a situation like this, and there was no manual on how to comfort people who had lost dear ones while on the run from an artificially intelligent system seeking their end. The only thing she could provide was sanctuary, and that was dependent on what the elders would say. She alone could not speak for everyone, she could count on her parent's support, but that may not be enough to convince the committee of elders who ran the community.

"Come, you passed out because of the shock and stress you experienced today. All of this was done on an empty stomach. You must be famished; you must eat. You are in luck; it's time for breakfast." Helen said with a smile as she walked out of the hut whilst motioning to them to follow her.

It was either because the food was delicious or due to their hunger that they found the food so enjoyable. They were, first of all, a bit apprehensive considering everything they were about to eat was natural and was cooked using wood as the source of heat. The moment they had their first bite, they immediately lost all form of etiquette and gorged on the food as if they hadn't eaten for weeks. Their actions caused some of the inhabitants to look down at them in disdain. The lefts had always been looked down on and in contempt by rights; this was a once in a lifetime opportunity for them to repay in kind. Other individuals had a different reaction when they saw the two eat in a manner uncharacteristic of the rights.

Some were full of smiles while watching them eat, others were surprised and disgusted that the so-called rights, for all their achievements and sense of superiority, would eat like animals. Food was supposed to be respected.

The atmosphere was disturbed by the sound of a Police siren in the distance, it was approaching rapidly and for a moment no-one knew what to do. Several children that were playing further out, ran towards the grand table shouting that the police had come and everyone immediately turned their gazes to Cayden and Stella. Helen immediately looked at her parents who signalled that she escorts them away, out the back door of the hut and towards the trees. Seeing that the community was willing to protect them, Cayden and Stella were filled with a feeling of deep appreciation towards the community, and as they left with Helen, Cayden mouthed a 'Thank you' to the elders.

"Wait, wait…we don't know if they are here for us or not. Let's wait and see what happens." Cayden suggested. Helen and Stella were at first against the idea, but he had a point. Their action was a little bit too presumptuous, assuming the police were here for them. Fear of Iris had caused their paranoia.

Two police cars pulled up in front of the grand table a few minutes after Cayden, Stella, and Helen had left and went to hide in the trees behind one of the huts. Patrolman Darren Forest came out of the first car.

"Hello, folks, Sorry to disturb you. I'm looking for these two."

The patrolman held up a poster showing photos of Cayden and Stella.

"I dropped them here last night, but a release was made on the police database that these two were on the run and were a threat to the general public. I do not need to ask if you have seen them, but are they still around?"

"That's the cop from last night. Look! He's got out pictures! How did they get it? We were careful not to show our faces. So how?" Stella exclaimed.

"Shhh! You are too loud! They will hear you." Cayden was quick to silence Stella. This was no time to wonder how they had given themselves up so quickly.

"Since it is clear they are here for you, I think it's best we leave." Helen said, not wanting to spend any more time in their present position. Any longer and they could be caught, and she would also be arrested as she might be accused of being an accomplice.

"Where do we go? This was the safest place we could think of. Your family and neighbours choose to live without the influence of modern technology. At first, I thought you were crazy, but if these past two days have taught me anything, it is that your family made the right decision." Stella silently cursed her situation.

Helen thought about it for a while, and she realized that Stella was right. She too could not think of a better and safer place than her home. Everywhere else had cameras and technology that could easily act as eyes for Iris to track their movement. Pondering on this fact, Helen started to wonder why exactly, was Iris after

Cayden and Stella. What exact threat did they present? It was highly likely they must have something that posed a threat to Iris. It had to be more than the fact that Iris had killed off their parents. Iris being sentient was not enough to cause mass panic, as it could be argued, that since she had been sentient, everything Iris had done was for the good of the planet.

Yes, Iris was supposed to protect humanity, but sacrificing those who were unproductive and a drain on resources in favour of those who made meaningful contributions to society seemed to make sense. Sadly, no morals were evident in Iris's 'thought process.' Decisions were made per each person's usual routine; hence, fewer people had to make decisions daily. Iris made the decisions for them. It was slowly turning humanity into mindless beings. Who was really the master? Taking everything into consideration, Helen felt there was something Cayden and Stella had either missed out on, or had deliberately with-held from her.

Thinking that the two might be hiding something from her, she pulled the two of them away from the hut and led them out of her community. When they were at a safe enough distance without any cameras in view, she stopped and looked both of them in the eye, her serious expression letting them know she wasn't going to accept any excuses or lies.

"What aren't you two telling me? This cannot possibly be because your parents died. You must have something that poses a threat to Iris. What is it?" Helen asked. This was no longer out of care but out of anger. She might potentially have put her family in harm's way while trying to befriend these two while they were still withholding information from her.

"We told you everything! There's nothing else left to tell you." Cayden shouted back. He was not as close to Helen as Stella was, so he did not have any problem being blunt with her.

"A-actually, that's not entirely true." Stella cut in. Her hands were shuffling through her clothes, a few seconds later, she brought out a device that looked like a brooch and handed it to Helen. As Stella brought out the device Cayden looked at Helen for her reaction, but to his surprise, she seemed more alarmed than confused as to what the device was.

"How did you get that?" She asked.

"What do you mean, how did we get that? Don't you mean what is that?" Cayden asked as he furrowed his eyebrows. "What is this? You clearly have a better understanding of what this is than we do."

"Tell us exactly what this is Helen?" Stella was no longer standing on formality any longer. This could explain why her parents had to die and why Iris had deemed them a threat to society. They initially thought it was because they had their chips destroyed, thereby making them an unpredictable variable.

"You all know about the mission to Mars 15 years ago? We sent a crew to construct a base, which was supposed to serve as a preliminary phase to foster the proliferation of humankind. Couples who had volunteered for the program were sent to start the initial stages of the colonization of Mars. Cayden interjected. "Of course, we remember. We sat up all night at my house watching it on the network. It was this that inspired us both to become astronauts."

"Well," Helen continued, "About 5 years ago we lost contact with them. I don't suppose your mother will mind me telling you this as it is supposed to be a secret." Helen's face looked saddened, as her thoughts of her mother's death seemed to be just sinking in now. However, she did seem to remember Jonathan telling them that NASA had lost the signal from the base on Mars.

"The funny thing was, we were still receiving updates through telemetry, but never actually spoke to a member of the crew. Jonathan built this device to receive emergency responses privately and I think it is also a type of flash drive."

Stella spoke up feeling quite intrigued.

"Why would Jonathan want to keep the messages secret?"

"According to your mother, he didn't want NASA to know what was going on so he developed this link directly with the Mars base."

"And why would he do that?"

"He thought that NASA's computers may have been compromised by Iris. The last message he received was a private message from a crew member called Calum Noble. He said that something had taken over their computers and had infiltrated the software of the robots. In effect, it was controlling the robots. He felt that his life was in danger as the robots seemed to be evolving at an alarming rate."

Cayden and Stella were stunned by the news and were frantically trying to connect the dots.

"But why would Iris target us because of this?" Cayden was still confused as to how this posed a threat to them. Helen looked at him intently.

"It would seem that Iris has now control over Primus and I'm willing to bet that this device will contain a 'kill code' that could erase the AI from the Cloud."

"But if that were the case why didn't my dad use it yesterday? There must be something else. Why is Iris after us?"

"Think about it this way, out of every individual on Earth, we three, besides my family and neighbours are probably the only individuals that do not have any chip implant. Iris can't see or hear what we talk about or do, neither can she track our movements. But, out of the three of us, only you two are capable of posing a real threat to Iris. Iris no longer knows what you know, It cannot afford to let you two move about freely," She paused as an afterthought entered her mind. "..and, you both are on the standby crew for the next trip to Mars."

Hearing Helen gave Cayden and Stella some sort of closure. They finally knew what the story behind the device and what its function was. However, they had no idea why either of their parents had it and why it was given to them.

"Your parents must have given it to you and placed it in your care for a reason. They would not give it to you without having a purpose. Or could it be..?" Helen had her speculations but could not be certain yet.

"Could it be what?" Stella asked.

"Thing is, your mother started to tell me, then she decided not to tell me the whole story, but she said she had overheard some government official talking about the possibility that the computer, that you both referred to as Iris, might have a mind of its own and that it might invariably put the crew on Primus in danger. They mentioned something about a restart code which would simply rewrite the building chains of the system, returning it to an older model of technology where services provided were limited."

"But, why would Iris, pose a threat to the folks up there?"

Cayden suddenly gave a gasp as he started to piece things together.

"I think I know what is going on." He was definitely his father's son when it came to solving puzzles.

"Dad didn't use the 'kill code' on the computer here because he knew it wouldn't get rid of Iris completely."

Helen anticipated Cayden's thoughts. "The Cloud or the machine's core is situated within the Mars base."

"Correct. Iris has moved to Mars." Stella was feeling a little naïve but had to ask why.

"For fear of any form of attack either physical or cyber or infiltration into the system by countries who may secretly attempt World domination." Cayden felt shocked at the enormity of the situation. Iris must have 'piggybacked' on one of the transmissions from NASA and had embedded itself in the computer and work-bots on Primus.

Hearing everything Helen said made it clearer to them why Iris had deemed them a threat and why their parents left the device in their care. They were to input this device into the computer core within the base on Mars.

"Your parents must have created the kill-code at the very last second and had no time to get it to Commander Alexander."

"Orion-3 is due to lift off tomorrow, maybe we can ask Commander Alexander to take the device to Primus and try to kill Iris with it." Stella was thinking fast as time was not their friend.

Cayden shook his head, "Nah, that won't work. Commander Alexander's implant will see everything. Iris will know what he is doing and might terminate him."

Stella agreed completely, why didn't she think of that. Iris and the Cloud were one. It could rule the Earth from its computer core on Mars like a God, unseen, untouchable and without recrimination. There were many unanswered questions. Would the kill-code work? Was the Cloud in the computer core on Primus or was it somewhere in cyberspace? Would the kill-code reach it?

"Sorry, Helen, but we will need your help."

Stella suddenly had a newfound resolve. She looked at Cayden and knew what it was their parents had tasked them with. It all made sense to them. She recollected the look on her parent's faces and now understood the look of happiness when they graduated. There was more to it than the pure joy of graduating and becoming an astronaut, it was hope. Both their parents looked to them as their new found hope of correcting their mistakes.

"What do you need me to do?" Helen asked as she became a little apprehensive regarding what Stella might ask her to do.

4 hours later

The three of them had managed to sneak into NASA. Helen knew every building, every corridor, and every alleyway and security post. They had changed their clothes and were in disguise, and so far everything was going to plan. Seeing as Helen and her kind refused the chip, they were given an emblem which was mandatory to wear whenever they were outside of their domain. She had gotten Stella and Cayden to dress as 'left cavemen' while wearing a cap to hide their faces. Iris had the capability for facial recognition, this was used Worldwide for making transactions, giving blood in the medical centre, and surveillance. They were not entirely sure, but when they noticed the cameras were not turning in their direction, they were pretty certain their plan was working.

They had managed to sneak into NASA and were hiding in the hanger as Helen walked freely into the building. She was tasked with granting them access into the building and then making her way through to the mission control area to initiate the launch sequence for the rocket. Her plan was to set off the fire alarm and wait until the staff had evacuated the building and mustered at the 'Assembly Point'. Helen took a deep breath, she felt like a criminal. There was something not quite right about vandalizing the 'Break Glass'. She had no time to ponder the morals of what she was about to do, and lifted her elbow and smashed it through the glass, setting off an almighty screech as the fire alarm sirens began wailing. Almost immediately, all of the staff downed tools and left their desks and consuls, the many fire drills they had practiced appeared to be worthwhile as the area was emptied of people within minutes. Taking advantage of the chaos Cayden and Stella made their way to the gantry that surrounded the Orion-3 and quickly entered the elevator that would take them up to the flight module. Beads of sweat started dripping from Cayden's brow as he pressed the button and waited for the elevator to start moving.

"Hello Cayden, hello Stella, your attempts will invariably prove useless. Did you honestly think I was unaware of your movements till now? Surrender now or face the consequence."

The moment they heard the voice, it felt like their hearts had been yanked out of their chests. Each time they heard Iris it was like its command of English was improving, it was difficult to tell now whether the voice was from an A.I. or from an actual human. They felt like pawns on a chessboard and had genuinely believed that they had outsmarted Iris. It turns out; she had been aware of their movements all along and was secretly allowing them access through the city. Had they paid attention while on the bus back into the right domain, they would have found it weird that the lights seemed to turn green just as they were approaching the sets of traffic lights they had encountered along the way.

"Cayden, what do we do?" Stella started to panic. Her earlier resolve had dissipated entirely.

Just as she was asking, the doors in the compound started to seal shut and the lights went red as the alarm went off. Helen, who had almost reached the control room, was startled when another alarm started blaring.

This was not the fire alarm, it was an intruder alert protocol, and was initiated by Iris. Rooms that were given 'priority one' were immediately sealed shut. This included the control room. The fire exit doors immediately opened automatically as workers continued to make their way out of the building. There was nothing Helen could do nothing anymore. The only ones who could enter the control room despite the fire protocol initiation were individuals with level 5 and above clearance. Sadly, she was only given a level 3 clearance.

"Damn! Had I been quicker!" Helen cursed silently.

There was nothing she could do now even if she wanted to. Everything was up to Cayden, and Stella who were no strangers to the protocol set by the facility. The moment the alarm went off, they knew they were on their own. They had failed. Stella felt a huge wave of disappointment wash over her. The memory of her parents smiling at her as she walked down the stairs on the day of her graduation was still fresh in her mind; her parents who had entrusted her with this task would be disappointed at her failure. She broke down and started to weep but Cayden, seeing Stella cry, rushed to her side, and tried to comfort her. Why did everything have to be controlled by Iris? He remembered his father talking about the good old days when his grandfather would teach his father how to drive a stick shift car. His father admitted he was a terrible learner and could never get it right, not the first time anyway. However, Cayden remembered the look he saw in his father's eyes as he related the story. He could see a quiet resolve and a determination to succeed in everything he did. A fighting spirit that Cayden had inherited. "That's it! Stella, I know what we can do." Cayden suddenly sprung to up, helping Stella up in the process. She was confused, she could see in Cayden's eyes a sense of madness and he looked like he was completely possessed as he forced the elevator door open.

"Where are we going?"

Stella had to ask. She had never seen Cayden like this. She started to wonder if the stress of it all had gotten to him. Was he losing it? She started to worry.

"The stairwell! Stella, the stairwell!"

Cayden shouted. As soon as she heard those words, she knew what he meant. There was hope! She had completely forgotten that the Orion-3 was not as big as the previous versions. The door to the flight command module was within climbing distance. They scampered up the gantry stairs as fast as they could until they reached the level that would bring them to the door of the ship. This Orion was far superior to the older models, the design was more futuristic, a triangular shape like something out of a science fiction movie. The anti-gravity propulsion system was the first of its kind, the theory being that it would reverse gravity and use the gravitational force to push the craft in any direction in space. On each side of the triangle, shaped craft there were thrusters that could be engaged to alter course, whilst the interior of the craft was built inside a gyroscopic bubble, a rotatable body that could maintain its stability for the crew. Even in the event of acute changes of direction at very fast speeds, the effects would be minimized so as not to disorientate crewmembers. In space, the Orion-3 could punch its way through a vacuum using (ZPE), Zero-point energy principles so there was little requirement to carry tons of fuel.

The ship was attached to rocket thrusters that would help it to escape from the Earth's atmosphere, these would be discarded after the first burn as the 'first stage', like the old Saturn rockets did in the 20th. Century. This was to be its maiden flight and Stella hoped that her years of training on the simulator would pay off. The Orion-3 had been tested and prepped and was ready for Commander Alexander and his crew's flight to Mars. The thought of it made Stella feel a tinge of regret at robbing the Commander of his mission, but her mission was more important.

"Where is it though?" Stella asked. She was no longer being pulled along, but she was running side by side on the gantry walkway with Cayden. This was another opportunity that had been gifted to her and she could not afford to fail again. Within minutes, the door to the Orion-3 flight module was within view.

"Your attempts are futile. Surrender now. Your end is imminent. You will be terminated."

Cayden and Stella paid no heed to Iris and its threats as they opened the door of the spacecraft.

"Wait, do you know how to pilot this ship?!"

Stella suddenly had a question as they boarded. Cayden laughed.

"You're kidding! A bit late to worry about that now. I've been ready for years."

Although the ship was not directly connected to the Cloud it could be controlled either manually or automatically. Onboard computers could do most of the tasks but, there were still aspects of the craft that indirectly linked the ship to the Cloud. Cayden knew that his father had built a firewall around NASA's computers and for the meantime, he felt they were relatively safe. If Iris had fully integrated into NASA's computers they would have been dead by now. The fact that they weren't was proof enough that Iris hadn't completely broken through yet and was still working its way into the system.

"Put on your suit!" Cayden instructed Stella. There was no need for a response. Getting to Mars would be the perfect reply.

"Security personnel will have been alerted by now. Probably be here at any moment." Cayden shouted as he hurriedly strapped himself in and started to go through the pre-flight check-list. He took one look at it and threw it over his shoulder.

"No time for this rigmarole." He reached over to the many flashing controls on the consul in front of him.

"Disengage clamps." He could see out of his window that the gantry was pulling away from the ship.

"Stella, are you ready? Do you have your suit secure?"

Stella looked over and gave him the 'thumbs up' sign. Cayden was trying to remember everything he was taught during training. It seemed easy at the time, but now he was not so sure. Perhaps he should have paid more attention.

"Cayden?" Stella called out to him.

"Not now," He replied.

"Cayden!" She screamed at him.

"What?!"

She pointed to a green flashing button that had LAUNCH written on it and the moment he hit the button, engines roared, the lights within the ship dimmed. Cayden and Stella took deep breaths in preparation of the G force that they expected would push them back into their chairs as they left Earth's atmosphere. They waited in anticipation of the surge, but they were going nowhere fast. The expected 'Lift Off.' was not happening.

"Futile attempt, Surrender."

"Cayden? What's wrong with the Orion? The launch sequence is not being initiated." Stella started to panic.

"What? Move aside; let me see. Crap! I'll be right back. Don't go anywhere!"

Cayden could see an infinite loop of repeated codes and immediately knew what was happening. Iris had gotten into the Orion system and was preventing them from leaving Earth. Time was of the essence, if either of them did nothing, the Orion would temporarily be unable to leave Earth. Iris was rewriting the codes used to program the Orion ship. If the codes inputted by Cayden and Stella differed from the code the Orion was programmed to take off with, the ship would be immediately shut down and be unable to take off. This was a defense mechanism taken by NASA to prevent possible theft of the Orion ship, even remotely. It was one of a kind and therefore, could not be allowed to fall into any hands other than NASA's.

"Ah! There it is!" Cayden ran back from the back of the ship with a small device that resembled a flash drive. He immediately inserted it into one of the numerous ports.

"What's that? What are you doing?" With everything going on, Stella felt left out and knowing information could be the fine line between life and death, she could not afford to drag both of them down with her ignorance. She immediately felt useless even though she knew this was not Cayden's intentions.

"It is a flash drive" Cayden replied as he frantically typed on the system.

"I know what it is Cayden; I am asking you what's going on? What are you doing? What's happening?" The frustration had reached its peak for her. She could not take it anymore, as the tone of her voice conveyed the anger she felt.

Cayden looked at her and immediately motioned to her to be quiet by placing his finger over his mouth. He could not afford to let Iris know what was happening. It was already in the Orion system and there was no telling how deeply it had integrated itself into the ship's computers. He could not afford Iris finding out what he was doing. So far, he knew it had not gained complete control of the ship. If it had, it would have immediately fought back against him. The moment it would gain control of the cameras, it would see what Cayden was doing, but so far, their luck was holding out.

Stella was angry, but she could only hold it back. She felt Cayden was doing what he always did, even now that their lives were in danger, and 'He was still focused on being the centre of attention. Who was here to watch? It was just the two of them,' she thought.

"Thank goodness I was not too late. I think I've done it." Cayden sighed with relief. He looked up at Stella and smiled. He knew her personality well. When he motioned to her to be quiet, he already knew what her reaction would be, but considering the urgency of the situation, Stella's feelings were the last thing he had on his mind.

"Iris is hacking into the Orion system and is preventing the launch sequence from initiating. It must have changed the launch sequence codes, and we don't know the new code. We have to match those codes to acknowledge the launch instruction. If we get it wrong, we won't be able to leave Earth at all. All other ships are directly linked to the Cloud except the Orion-3. I think Iris was only able to get on because the Orion is linked to NASA's system temporarily for the launch codes to be sent prior to launch."

He looked over at Stella and smiled, before boastfully announcing.

"I was able to get in there first. I had to insert the firewalls, but I could not risk Iris finding out, that was why I had to silence you."

"Can we leave now?"

Stella asked. It was apparent she was still angry. She understood why Cayden did what he did, but she still felt a slight resentment towards his actions. It would take her a while before she got over it.

"Not yet. I have to input the codes." Cayden replied. He had that look on his face that indicated he was in command.

"Okay? What's the problem? The guards will be here any moment." Stella was past scared at this point. The alarm had been blaring for a while now and in a couple of minutes, the armed guards would be here, and their route would be closed off.

"Oh shit! Iris was able to change one of the codes. I don't know which of the 14 digit codes were changed."

As much as they both wanted to leave, they could not afford to be impulsive and jeopardize everything. The atmosphere immediately became gloomier. They had sacrificed so much, and yet this was the outcome? They could not afford to initiate the launch sequence codes they were given in the pre-flight training at the academy for fear the first code could be the wrong code. If that was the case, forget taking off, there was no point inserting the remaining codes.

A beeping sound was heard from the flight consul and the numbers on the screen scrambled until it read 00000015.00.

"What does that mean?" Stella shouted. As if to answer her question, Iris's voice boomed over the sound system.

"Automatic self-destruct initiated. Countdown commencing."

Cayden knew their time was up. Iris was going to destroy the ship in 15 minutes. He looked over at Stella, her angst-ridden expression told him everything. He slowly walked over to her and hugged her as tight as he could, no words were spoken, just an understanding they both had, they had failed, but at least, they failed together.

"14 minutes to automatic self-destruct."

Cayden looked out the window, he could see the security guards running towards the exits, trying to get as far away as possible from the expected explosion. The sight of the men running for their lives seemed to revive his fighting spirit.

"C'mon Stella, we've got to try and find a way to stop this. You take the onboard computer controls and I'll try to hack it from inside."

Stella sprang into action and started to punch codes into the computer while Cayden used what knowledge he had to figure out a way to circumvent the system. Suddenly, loud music started blaring out of the sound systems. It was songs all related to their present predicament.

"We gotta' get out of this place if it's the last thing we ever do."

"The Animals." Cayden shouted.

"The what?" Stella called out, as her voice was barely audible above the loud music.

"The Animals, a British group from the 1960s."

"Just like him." Stella mused, "Still acting childishly, even though our lives are in danger.

The loud music continued and Cayden shouted out the names of the artists as if it were some kind of a deadly game.

"Is there life on Mars?"

"Bowie."

"I'm a rocket man."

"Elton John."

Stella couldn't contain her frustration at Cayden's behaviour and threw a pencil and paper at him. "Can you just not do that!"

"4 minutes to automatic self-destruct."

The irritation of the loud music had Stella clutching her ears, it was hard enough to concentrate let alone try to work out a way to stop the self-destruct. Cayden, on the other hand, was singing along while trying input a code that would cancel the danger.

"I can't." Stella mumbled as she slumped to the floor.

"I'm done." Cayden stopped what he was doing and sat beside her, finally accepting defeat. He held her hand and looked at her lovingly.

"I'm sorry it will end like this. I had so many plans for us." Stella wiped a tear from her eye with her sleeve.

"Don't be sorry, I've loved every minute I've spent with you. I have no regrets." The two sat motionless as the loud music persisted and seemed to permeate every nook and cranny of the ship. Was this some kind of sick humour from Iris or was it merely trying to distract them from trying to find a way to cancel the self-destruct?

"3 minutes to automatic self-destruct."

----

36 hours earlier

Jonathan, Henry, and Jasmine are cradling the unconscious Cayden and Stella on the stairwell. A few moments earlier, they had zapped the two with a special EMP that had rendered their implants inoperative.

"We have to do this to ourselves if we want to hide from Iris." Jonathan said in his usual authoritative manner.

"Quick, I've prepared a shot for each of us that will release us from our implants. C'mon Let's do this before Iris becomes aware of what we are doing."

Jonathan proceeded to zap Henry and Jasmine who fell unconscious in front of him but before he turned it on himself, he slipped a small device into one of Stella's pockets and then turned the small pulse gun on himself.

"Good luck guys." He whispered before blackness engulfed him.

Jonathan had ensured that Cayden and Stella had been given a more powerful dose of the EMP than they had, so that they would be unconscious for a longer period. Thus, giving the parents time to recover more rapidly. First, to recover was Henry, then Jasmine, then Jonathan.

"I feel so lonely, so cut off from everything. I feel vulnerable." Jasmine complained as Henry helped her to her feet.

"You will get used to it.' Jasmine turned to look at the unconscious figures of their two children.

"Jonathan, we can't leave them like this."

"We have to. They are in more danger with us than they are on their own."

Henry agreed, "He's right Jasmine. We cannot stay with them. Iris is out of control. The kids should believe we are dead. Iris thinks we are dead; it makes it easier to take her down from the shadows."

"Jasmine, I am sorry. If we do this right, we will get to see them again. Let's go. There's an underground tunnel that was built by my father. We will use that to escape. I have a place we can go to, it's a bit archaic, but it keeps us out of the Cloud. C'mon! Let's go."

Jonathan spoke as his gaze never let Cayden. He felt immense sorrow leaving Cayden like this. He knew how much Cayden blamed himself for the death of his mother and how lonely he felt because of it. He knew what his actions could do to Cayden, but he had to. It was for their own good and that of everyone in the

World. The only consoling factor was Stella. Watching Stella's unconscious body next to Cayden's gave him some sort of comfort, as he knew his son would not be alone in all of this. As they hurried down the stairwell, Henry questioned Jonathan about the underground tunnel.

"My father built it in the early days of his AI experiments. Off one of the tunnels is a small room that he built to be used as a safe house or a panic room in case there was ever a terrorist attack or some kind of emergency. Those were the days when officials in the dark corridors of power could selectively control a person's brain function by transcranial magnetic stimulation TMS. This technique used powerful pulses of electromagnetic radiation that was beamed into a person's brain, usually through their cell phone, to instruct them to commit all types of atrocities."

"Really?" Henry was quite impressed by the Gray family's ingenuity.

"Yes, my father was, what should I say, a follower of conspiracy theories, and surprisingly some of those theories have turned out to be true.

"Like?" Henry gasped as he took a quick breath, the ground floor seemed much further away when using the stairs.

"In the early part of the century the Federal Network Agency auctioned frequencies that would allow high data rates and faster speeds. It was for the new 5G network, the new generation of mobile internet connectivity. Transmitters and receivers were situated all over the planet. It was the real start of the surveillance culture. My father got involved when reports of birds falling from the sky and people complaining about severe headaches began to appear. He thought the electromagnetic radiation emanating from these frequencies had something to do with the 5G, but the experts told him that 5G produced less electromagnetic radiation than he would receive on a sunny day. However, he thought this a bit of a cop out, and thought the real benefit from 5G was the ability to get into peoples' heads. Thankfully, those days have gone since Iris came online. Nowadays, within each person's implant, there is a firewall which can stop any intrusion into an individual's brain."

The group reached the ground floor and ran towards the entrance to the basement, then proceeded down another set of stairs that led them to the tunnel. Jasmine began to feel her legs aching, the bad smell from the tunnel was nauseating, and the sound of water dripping from the roof and splashing to the ground made her even more uncomfortable.

"How much further?" she complained. Jonathan stopped and opened a small panel on the tunnel wall.

"We are here now." He looked into the panel expecting the door to open but nothing happened. "Of course, my implant won't work." He said somewhat exasperated. He dug deep into his pockets under his lab coat and produced an old-fashioned key. Henry was amazed at what he saw inside the basement. There were old newspapers strewn across the tables, unusual because newspapers hadn't been used for years, these days, everybody relied on their implants for news feeds. He noted a number of computers and keyboards on the tables and a huge computer mainframe tucked in the corner.

"Wow!" He exclaimed as he pointed to the mainframe. "That's old. I could probably get more from a microchip the size of my fingernail than what I could get out of that thing."

Jonathan looked over at him, "I've been working on it and made a few enhancements." and started to clear the mess off the table.

"My father used an older computer system that is now obsolete, but I'm pretty sure that will turn out to be a bonus. He had encrypted firewalls for protection that hopefully Iris will not be able to penetrate. I've been working here, now and again, and have been using it to monitor the Mars expedition. I've also been keeping an eye on the Orion-3, just out of interest. Saves me going to NASA to watch."

Henry was quite impressed with his boss's work ethic and more importantly, he felt that he had a safe place to hide. Jasmine sat on one of the chairs, still out of breath from her exertions, as Jonathan hurried over to a power unit on the wall.

"No time for resting, we have worked to do." And with that, he pulled the lever down with a clunk. A faint whirring sound was heard and lights started flashing around the room signaling that Jonathan's computers were booting up, ready to be used.

Cayden and Stella had resigned themselves to their fate, even the noise from the songs being played by Iris seemed to drift into the background. They had minutes left before the unthinkable would happen when something on the countdown timer caught her attention. The numbers started flashing randomly. Something was happening. She noticed codes were being inputted into the system automatically.

"What is it?" Cayden asked. Still sitting on the floor with his back against the wall. He had already felt defeated and had given up hope completely.

"Come take a look at this," Stella said in a somewhat excited but perplexed tone. Cayden immediately got up and launched himself to the control panel. He saw exactly what Stella was seeing. The codes were being inputted remotely. They both looked at each other with confused expressions on their faces. What was going on? Was this another of Iris's bad attempts at humour. At that exact moment, the loud music stopped.

"Could it be.." Stella was about to ask when Cayden cut in.

"N-no. It's not possible. Iris no longer has any control over the system. It's trying to prevent us from leaving Earth. Why then would it help us?" Cayden knew this was definitely not Iris. There was no one they knew on the outside that was able to help them.

"Wait! Do you think Helen...?" Stella asked in a somewhat elated manner.

"Hmmm..." Cayden said nothing more than that. He knew there was no way Helen would know the codes. Only a few people were chosen to know the launch sequence codes, and they were not allowed to share it. Cayden had been chosen on account of his father. The other chosen individuals had important people as their guarantors and would never divulge the information, they had all signed the confidentiality agreement, and therefore, could never disclose any secrets. To do so would be considered as treason.

'Who could it be?' Cayden thought to himself.

"Launch sequence initiated, prepare for lift-off."

Stella could no longer hold it in anymore. She was ecstatic as the both of them immediately got into their respective seats and strapped themselves in.

"Quick, get your helmet on."

Stella didn't need to be told twice as she was already in the process of latching it on. The vibration was a lot more than she had expected as she looked through her visor at Cayden who was busily pressing buttons and flicking switches.

"Inertial Mass Reduction, active." Stella had dreamed about going to space, but had hoped it would have been under more pleasant circumstances.

"I hope he knows what he is doing." She said to herself, all the time feeling very proud of his efforts at trying to fly this magnificent machine.

"He has done all the training as a co-pilot so should be able to manage." She murmured as she tried to remain positive. Suddenly the G-force pinned them back in their seats as they felt the upward thrust of the Orion-3 blasting it's way like a silver bullet to escape velocity.

"Did they make it out, okay?"

Henry and Jasmine had worried looks on their faces as they asked Jonathan. Jonathan reclined on his chair as he removed his glasses and rubbed his eyes. It was now that they realized just how scared he was earlier. They had always been monitoring their kids. They were parents; it was in their job description to know where their kids were. They were underground, and the technology was archaic compared to what they were used to, but the beauty of it was, it was not connected to anything. There was no way for Iris to track them or attack their location. They were completely off the grid. This was where Jonathan had been working on a kill-code that could combat Iris and hopefully succeeded in eliminating its conscious system.

"Yes, they did. There's so little we can do for them at this point. All we can hope is that they stay safe and are careful." Jonathan said as he got up and walked across the room to an old musty couch to rest.

"But Mars is extremely dangerous. The robots are.."

Henry held Jasmine's hands as he tried to stop her from saying anything any further. He knew best how stressed and worried Jonathan was. He had barely slept since this whole thing started a few days ago. He understood his wife's feelings, but he also could not be selfish and only care about his daughter, Jonathan's son was also with his daughter. If he wanted Cayden safe, then it invariably meant he wanted Stella safe too. Jasmine realizing the motive behind her husband's action was a little taken back. Was he more concerned about Jonathan's feelings than their daughter? She felt slightly betrayed.

Henry seeing the look his wife shot him, could only shake his head at how temperamental his wife was. She had become so overwhelmed with her emotions that she failed to see the hurt on Jonathan's face. They were all to blame for the present situation they were in. Jonathan was a long-time friend to them and was the one to give them their respective job positions when they barely had enough. Her actions were like a slap in his face. Henry got up and headed over to Jonathan. Seeing her husband's actions and the look on Jonathan's face, Jasmine felt somewhat bad. She had lost herself in the heat of the moment. Days and weeks of burying herself at work to take her mind off the fear and imaginary thoughts she had towards her daughter had caused a lot of pent up frustration that was released the moment she knew her daughter was still alive and in trouble. She could only cry. This was the only thing she had left to do. She missed her daughter. "Mum." What she would give to hear those words again; to be called that again.

CHAPTER 5

High above the Earth Cayden and Stella felt the relief as the G-force subsided. For a moment, they both sat quietly with their thoughts. The Earth looked so beautiful, so serene. It was hard to imagine that this beautiful planet was beset with so many problems. Suddenly, their daydreams were cruelly interrupted by the sound of a buzzer which seemed to resonate through the whole ship.

"Oh no, what's that?" Stella's moment of calm was over. Cayden scanned the consul looking for a warning light to establish what caused the alarm.

"No, not now, damn it."

"Tell me. What is it?"

"We are not reaching the speed we should. Something is causing a drag. If we don't make it to the point where we set our trajectory for Mars we could be in trouble."

Cayden frantically looked around, trying to find out what was causing the drag when he noticed the sign that showed a successful disengagement of the 'first stage' booster was not illuminated.

"I've found the problem." He shouted to the anxious Stella. The 'first stage' booster was supposed to have disengaged automatically after the initial thrust, but for some reason, it hadn't separated from the ship and now the extra weight and friction was slowing the Orion down."

"Now what do I do?" Cayden was exasperated and all out of ideas. He looked over at the forlorn face of Stella. A deep feeling of anger and regret engulfed him. He felt he had failed her. She didn't deserve this. As if to get rid of all his pent-up frustration he raised his fist and slammed it forcefully on the consul.

"Damn!"

Almost immediately, they felt a slight jolt, and as if by some miracle the 'Booster Disengaged' light was now illuminated. Cayden looked out of his window and could see the 'first stage' boosters falling back to Earth.

"You did it. I knew you could." Stella whooped. Cayden knew he hadn't done anything, it was just a coincidence that the booster separated when he banged his fist on the table, but if Stella wants to think it was him who solved the problem, who was he to spoil the moment.

"Stella, switch to autopilot," Cayden instructed. "We should be able to take our helmets off now."

"The Orion has not been fully tested yet. Maybe we should go through the systems and check that everything is in order. There should be enough food to last us for the journey." Cayden said as he got up and headed into the mini kitchen. There was only a sink and a machine that was the same height as a vending machine. It had a keyboard that allowed its user type in whatever food they desired and it would be made right there and then. This was one of the many perks of living in a technologically advanced World.

"Do you want anything?" Stella was still at her seat completely lost in thought. Tears were streaming down her cheeks as she stared at a picture. It was a picture of herself and her parents. Memories flooded through her mind as she thought back to when things were simple. She remembered her home, her room, her 'elite' lifestyle, and the times she would go over to Cayden's house as a child, those times were simple. Ignorance was truly bliss. Feeling very teary and emotional, she unstrapped herself from her seat and walked over to the small sleeping accommodation, and sat on the side of a bunk bed.

"Hey, hey, what's wrong?" Cayden asked as he approached her. He could hear her crying. When he saw the picture in her hands, he was involuntarily reminded of those simple times. One person was constant through all his thoughts, his father. He missed him a lot.

"They are gone, Stella, there's nothing we can do to bring them back. What we should be focusing on is surviving. It is what they would have wanted." As Cayden spoke, the impact of the words he had uttered suddenly hit him. Their parents were gone. They were alone. They only had each other.

"No! They cannot be gone!" Stella could not hold it anymore as she broke down in tears. From the moment they woke up till now, it had been one thing or another. They had been continually running; reality had not yet dawned on them. However, at this precise moment, in the stillness of space, they actually felt safer than they had been over the last couple of days. It was quiet, they were utterly alone; Iris was no longer a threat, at least not for now.

Cayden watched Stella let out all her pain and pent up emotions. He felt completely helpless. There was nothing he could do. He moved towards her and when she saw him coming close to her, she could not help herself anymore, she launched herself into his embrace and hugged him tightly while letting out a deep sigh. Cayden did nothing but hold her throughout the whole time she cried until she fell asleep. When she woke up, she and Cayden were both on the bed. She turned over and saw him sleeping next to her. Seeing this caused her to smile. For a second there, she thought her nightmare had become a reality. She believed she was truly alone. Everyone in her life had died. She moved closer to Cayden and held him tightly. Reality had finally dawned on her that she only had one person left, and that was Cayden; she could not afford to lose him.

Cayden opened his eyes. He was still next to Stella and had absolutely no idea of the time. All he knew was that he felt refreshed and must have slept for around 8 hours. He didn't want to waken her, she looked so peaceful in her slumber, but he had to. After breakfast, which consisted of a mash-up of sausage and egg, Cayden started to make plans for their hibernation, which would last for 5 months. The ship was equipped with cryo-pods, which would keep them asleep for most of the journey.

"Well, it's time." Cayden smiled, as he knew this was the last time he would see her for 5 months. "Time to get you plugged in."

These were the new cryo-pods, and weren't really cryogenic, as experiments with freezing volunteers for an extended period of time had not been successful. Many of the people who had gone on trials with the original cryogenic pods never woke up, and those that did had brain damage. Some doctors had reported that patients were kept in a nightmare that kept looping over and over again, resulting in them, being retarded when they were woken up.

"Don't worry Stella, you'll be in cryo-sleep in no time." Cayden reassured her as she stepped into the pod. "I just have to slow down your heartbeat and drop your body temperature slightly." Cayden wanted to make sure that Stella knew exactly what he was doing. "This is called Torpor, something that is done by animals as a survival tactic in winter, a type of light hibernation. This system has now been adopted by NASA rather than freezing." Cayden explained as he prepared the tubes to be inserted into Stella's arm.

"I will join you as soon as I see that you are asleep." Stella just smiled at him. In some ways, she was looking forward to hibernating.

Just as Cayden was preparing the cryo-sleep pods, the alarm sounded on the ship's consul.

"What next?" he grumbled. Stella had heard the alarm too and climbed out of the pod to join Cayden at the control panel.

"Another problem?"

"Looks like we are way off course."

The room was dark apart from the flashing lights from the computers, and the constant whirring sound served as a kind of relaxation and meditation for stress relief. Jonathan was fast asleep on the old couch while Henry and Jasmine shared a blanket on the floor. The calmness was about to be disturbed by an intermittent beeping sound coming from one of the computers.

The alarm woke them all up. Jonathan was the quickest. He knew what the alarm signified; this was the one sound he dreaded having to hear. Their kids were in trouble. He ran to his computer and frantically started typing a series of code.

"Jonathan, what's wrong?" Henry was next up.

"I do not know yet, but it sounds like trouble."

Hearing those words caused all three parents to panic. They had all visibly aged. Jonathan was the worst out of the three. He was now a far cry from what he looked like before the crisis started. He had appeared to age, at the very least, by ten years. He frantically hit the buttons on the computer. Henry quickly followed as they both tried to see what the problem was.

"Oh, no." Henry pulled away from the computer. He had his hands over his mouth. His actions caused both Jonathan and Jasmine's hearts to sink. They had already envisioned the worst possible case scenario.

"What is it!? Is Stella, okay!?" Jasmine quickly asked but immediately regretted her words when she saw Jonathan glance at her. How could she only be concerned about her daughter forgetting Cayden was also involved? "..and Cayden?" She self-consciously asked.

"I did not notice at the time. It is my fault." Henry seemed not to have heard Jasmine's question.

"What is it, Henry?" Jonathan was also anxious. When he helped Cayden and Stella earlier, he immediately logged out of the system to avoid Iris noticing any interference.

"When Iris tampered with the launch codes on the vessel, it also tampered with the automatic control system." Henry had calculated that Iris had managed to delay the automatic separation of the 'first stage' booster resulting in them slowing down and not reaching their intersection point on the Mars trajectory. Jonathan had already uploaded the co-ordinates to the Orion-3 to compensate for the early lift-off but somehow the automatic navigation system hadn't applied the changes. The Orion-3 had missed the vital point where they were to have changed course. Henry turned to Jonathan and Jasmine.

"They've been heading in the wrong direction for god knows how long."

"What!? Where are they headed?" Jasmine asked. Her face had gone pale. The past couple of months have been tough on her. She had long since passed her limitations.

"They are heading nowhere. From the looks of it, Iris must have messed up their navigation system and based on what I can see, there's no way they are aware of it. They are heading out into oblivion with no idea that they are stranded."

Henry felt a surge of anger within him. How much more could they take. For months, they've lived a life they were not proud of because of Iris. Regret was what Jonathan, Henry, and Jasmine were feeling at this point. They were the creators of Iris. It was designed to solve many of humanity's problems. It was designed to amass data, and with it, act based on a series of algorithm designed by Jonathan. It was supposed to take humanity to the next level of evolution. What they didn't count on was that Iris would deem humanity as its enemy as well as its friend. Where did Iris stand in all this? Could Iris be inadvertently destroying humanity with its efforts to save the planet? Jonathan blamed himself for Iris's actions.

"If only I had made a clear comparison on the program about saving the planet, protecting humanity and not to harm humans. I didn't spend enough time on ethical behavior. I was so sure that the more Iris evolved, the more compassionate it would be. I was wrong." These were the thoughts that had haunted him ever since the Cloud had become sentient.

Hearing what Henry said, Jonathan summoned what little strength he had left and frantically started typing on the computer in front of him.

"What are you..? If you do that.." Henry immediately realized what Jonathan was doing.

"Do you have a better idea!? You would rather stay hidden and safe, than save your daughter from dying!?" Jonathan roared back at Henry.

Jasmine at first did not understand what Jonathan was doing until she saw the exchange between her husband and Jonathan. Did she understand that their life of relative safety was coming to an end?

"First of all, the least I can do is alert them. Secondly, undo what Iris did to the navigation system. I don't know how far out they are from Earth or Mars, but it's highly unlikely they will have enough fuel and supplies to make it to Mars, let alone a return trip to Earth."

"You want them stranded on Mars knowing full well what's happened on Primus!?" Jasmine could not take it anymore. She was okay being treated like she did not exist provided; if it was in the best interest of everyone, but what Jonathan was proposing was essentially suicide for her daughter.

"What else do you suggest!?"

Jonathan had had enough. He had listened to Jasmine act as though she was the only one losing a child. Cayden was up there with Stella, yet she did not care so much about his life, only Stella's.

"What do you want from me, Jasmine!? We do not get to pick and choose! It's either they are stranded in Space and die or Mars. They cannot come back to Earth. The moment I attempt to correct their navigation system, Iris will be aware of our existence. Do you want them coming to Earth then? It will immediately know of their arrival, and that makes it easier for Iris to deal with them. Mars is the only choice of survival for them." He was equally angry and frustrated. Who was Jasmine to make it seem like he did not care about his son?

"Jasmine pack everything. Once Jonathan does this, we'll have to leave here immediately. The moment he attempts to hack into the Orion-3, Iris will detect his actions and will be made aware that we are alive. We need to leave here now!"

Henry's tone was firm to Jasmine. He was not happy the way Jonathan spoke to Jasmine, but he also understood that everything Jonathan said was the truth. They could not think of any other alternative.

"First things first, Cayden and Stella need to be aware that they are going the wrong way."

"What will you do?" Jasmine asked from the room as she started packing.

"I'll reset the navigation system and raise the alarm on the ship." His words seemed casual, but in his heart, Jonathan felt very worried about the situation. He had no hesitations when it came to saving Cayden and Stella. However, the risk it posed to himself, Henry and Jasmine was not something he could overlook.

An hour later, Jonathan got off the computer and slumped on the couch. His head bowed and a feeling of weariness had taken over his earlier feelings of enthusiasm and optimism.

"Is it done?" Henry asked.

"Yes. It will take a while before the signal reaches them, however, once they discover what's wrong, hopefully, they will know what to do." Jonathan replied, with a hint of despair in his voice. "I think we'd better form a plan, a strategy, we're going to need one if we want to keep hidden from Iris." He sat back down on the couch, his head in his hands hiding the teardrop that had ran down his cheek. The room had suddenly become quiet again as the respective parents were deep in thought, no doubt reminiscing about the days when they were all together, laughing, playing and enjoying life. It was the feeling of utter helplessness that was affecting them the most.

Henry was the first to break the silence.

"I suppose we could always go 'below the belt' and join Helen in the 'Caveman' community. At least we will be safe from Iris there." Jasmine just glanced at him with one of her lofty looks of disdain.

"I'd rather stay in our summer cabin, it's not too far away. If I'm going to be a hermit then I'd rather stay in my own place." Henry nodded in agreement.

"Could be cold in the winter though, but I'm sure we could survive the elements..." His sentence wasn't finished as Jonathan stood up quickly thumping his fist into the palm of his hand. It was like a eureka moment.

"Elements, exactly." He had this excited look in his eyes, a look that had been missing for some time now. He smiled at Henry. "Well done Henry."

"What did I do?"

"You gave me the answer, elements." Henry was still a little confused, what exactly did Jonathan have in mind. He looked over to his friend hoping for an explanation. By this time, Jonathan was frantically searching through the cabinets and desk drawers, before settling down in front of one of the computers. He typed furiously until he found what he was looking for.

"That's it, Element 115." For the slightest moment, Henry had thought his friend had finally snapped until he also started to remember.

"Space-time Compression? He blurted out excitedly. "I thought Element 115 was too unstable?"

"It is, but recent research has found ways to stabilize it and to harness the energy for future propulsion systems."

"How is this going to affect Stella and Cayden? I don't see it." For a moment, Henry appeared confused, but he knew Jonathan was always one step ahead. He was, after all, the owner of the World's biggest technological company.

The change of mood had aroused Jasmine's interest, but she had no idea what they were talking about this time. This must have been top-secret stuff if she hadn't heard about it, as she prided herself in having her ear to the ground, so to speak, or in other words knowing what gossip was going around the tech industry.

Jonathan swiveled his chair round to face Henry and Jasmine. It was time to lay his cards on the table.

"You guys know that we work with the government, right? Well, one of the projects we have been working on is the anti-matter reactor fueled by Element 115. It is to generate a gravity field for space-time compression. If it works we will be able to reach speeds in space that would have, up until now, been unthinkable." Jasmine was trying to comprehend what Jonathan was saying, but this was way above her pay grade, all she was concerned about was, how was this going to help Stella and Cayden?

Seeing Jasmine's confused expression Jonathan explained.

"Commander Alexander was to conduct experiments with a new propulsion system based on the use of Element 115. They built a small reactor on the

Orion-3 and an interface to input the isotope containing the element. I think if Cayden and Stella can figure it out they might be able to use it to get back on course and shorten their journey time to Mars. Only one problem,"

"And that is?" Jasmine asked.

"The computers in this room won't be able to get through to the Orion-3 immediately, and by the time we do get through to them, they will have gone even further out into space. We have to go to NASA mission control and bounce a message off one of their satellites for direct face time. Of course, it will be highly likely that Iris will already have control of the ship."

Henry picked up his coat and hurried to the door. "What are we waiting for?" Jonathan switched off the power to the room, had one last look around before closing the door and locking it with the old key. Within minutes, he had caught up with the couple who were striding purposely through the damp, dark, wet, and smelly tunnel.

The past few days had been immensely tough for Jonathan, Henry, and Jasmine. Everything down to the basics was extremely difficult for them, including finding something to eat. They found themselves at a small roadside diner, but the problem was they had no money. They were so used to paying everything with their implant, and now that it was gone, they had no means to purchase food, but at least they were able to sit on a bench that was in the diner car park and rest their weary feet.

"I wonder why the Z-virus didn't clear Iris out of the system?" Jasmine asked. It was more of a thought than a question.

"I guess Iris and the Cloud have evolved enough to form some kind of self-defence, their own firewall to stop any intrusion into their system." Was the reply from Henry.

"I suspect that Iris has already found a way to integrate with the computer systems in NASA, and if that is true, it is only a matter of time before it uploads itself into the computer mainframe on Primus. Imagine, it could rule the World from another planet!"

Jonathan was thinking about the communication sphere given to Stella on the stairwell. At that time, it was a goodbye from them, but it wasn't a goodbye from Cayden and Stella, there was still unfinished business. He felt Cayden and Stella hadn't said their goodbyes and may still be alive, at least that was what he hoped. He had thought hard about telling Henry and Jasmine about the device he had inserted into one of Stella's pockets, but decided against it, as the fewer people who knew about it the better. The device was his only means of communication with crewmember Calum Noble on the Mars base. The last message he had received was very worrying and indicated that Iris may already be in control, however, the device he had inserted into Stella's pocket also contained a kill-code that he had created only moments before rushing to the stairwell. It was also based on self-learning software, and he hoped, it too, would evolve to match any further transitions by Iris. He looked at the sky. The sight was painful, the picture of a father yearning for his son. Tears were running down his cheeks. When he hacked into the Orion system to warn Cayden and Stella, he had determined where they were and realized just how far away they were from Mars. He had done the maths and realized there was no way the fuel could bring them back to Earth, let alone get to Mars.

It was night-time. Jonathan checked his watch; it was past midnight. "Get some sleep." That was all he had to say. They were camping in the field, a few miles away from the NASA launch site. They weren't alone however as this location was often used by on-lookers to view rocket launches from a safe distance. It was also, where Cayden and Stella had broken in to flee Earth on the spaceship Orion-3. Jonathan took one last look at the star-filled sky before entering his tent. As he lay on his back, thinking about what tomorrow's plan of action would be, he could hear Henry and Jasmine arguing. Their voices were getting louder, the more heated the argument got.

"What is his problem? These days, he has been getting more distant from us. He keeps to himself and does not tell us what is going on in his head. Did you know about the experiments with Element 115? What does he expect from us?"

"Shhh!... he will hear you."

"I don't care!"

"Jasmine! You need to look at it from his perspective. He lost his wife and the only person left for him is his son Cayden, who is now somewhere in space drifting away. We do not know how far away they are, not to mention, they have been headed in the wrong direction for the past couple of days. That's enough stress for him. He has no one left."

"I knew it! I just knew it. Why do you always have to stick up for him? You always have to suck-up to him. Do you want to play fetch as well? C'mon Henry! Our daughter, remember her? She is up there too." Her voice was no longer quiet. The more Henry tried to keep her quiet and calm, the more determined she was to get louder.

Jonathan heard the two but could not be bothered with their drama. He was furious with what Jasmine said. Could he now no longer grieve in peace? Stella, Stella, Stella, that was the only name she kept talking about all the time. He had a son too, but he never let that get to him. How dare she. Jonathan was about to step out to exchange words with Jasmine, but he decided against it. There was no point. Arguing would not bring them back or ensure their safety. If anything had happened to them, then the least they could do was ensure their children did not die in vain by destroying Iris on Earth. The problem was, if Iris has embedded itself on Primus it would only be a matter of time before it regained control of Earth's networks.

He looked one last time at the stars before he shut his tent door. He saw a shooting star and wondered one last time how his son was. Maybe he could see the same shooting star, the thought made him feel closer to his son as closed his eyes and slept what little sleep he could muster.

Consumers were those who the government had to take care of but were making no real contribution to the economy. Leeches, parasites, these were terms Iris classified them as. It would be a tragedy to have this group of humans proliferate anywhere. Death was the only answer for those classified as consumers as determined by Iris. This decision was based on their contribution to society, or lack of, lifestyle choices, tax payments, job, health issues, insurances, and the likes. Those that had green coloured left eyes, were deemed surplus to requirements, just as those in positions of power, and those who put their self-interests before the good of the planet. These were all parameters that contributed to the decisions taken by Iris. No one on Earth was more aware of this than the three individuals who had now just entered the NASA compound.

"Jonathan, where are we going?" Henry whispered. They were dressed as NASA personnel.

"Shhh...keep quiet. Act normal, will you? You look like you are up to something. Acting suspiciously will get us all caught. Relax!" Jonathan berated.

"Oh sorry, I don't go around sneaking into private facilities every other day. This is all new to me." Henry was a little annoyed with Jonathan's tone.

Jasmine watched the two and kept quiet. She realized her actions these past few days were unfair to Jonathan. She had been selfish, only thinking about herself and how she missed her daughter forgetting Jonathan was probably going through the same if not worse, considering Iris was his creation and idea.

"There, that's where we are going." Jonathan pointed to a particular room that was on the second top floor. The building was square-shaped, so it made it easy for him to point out their destination. The room they were headed for was facing them.

"What's there?" Jasmine asked. Her tone being friendlier than before.

"What we came here for." Although he noticed the slight change in Jasmine's actions and attitude towards him, it was still not enough to make him forget everything she had done and said to him.

Henry glanced at Jasmine to see her reaction only to notice she was not in the least bit affected by Jonathan's attitude. In truth, she would have found it more awkward if Jonathan had acted as though nothing had happened.

Walking with their heads down, Jasmine could not help but think back to when they were treated as welcome guests when they came here, but now, they were acting like convicts in the same place where they had been openly accepted. The irony of the situation hadn't escaped her.

After Jonathan had purged Iris from the Orion-3, enabling Cayden and Stella to escape, it had been alerted to their existence. They were now wanted and were high on the priority list from humanity's heroes to becoming wanted criminals. The plummet in social status was suicidal.

They needed passes to get into the room, but luckily the locker Jonathan broke into belonged to an employee who had the required access into such a place. It was lunch break and a lot of the staff were not in their offices, most were busy relating with their colleagues at the kitchens on each floor. Life here was built for the comfort of the staff primarily.

Jonathan swiped the stolen ID card. "We are in." he whispered.

"Iris doesn't seem to have spotted us. The alarm hasn't gone off so, seems no one is aware of our presence, yet." Henry added. In truth, they were worried about this. Things were going smoothly, too smoothly though. Everything seemed to be working out for them: it was borderline divine intervention.

"That's the computer over there. Henry, I'll need you to break down the network defense and at the same time try as much as possible not to leave any trace for Iris to follow. Drop pseudo baits for her."

For some reason, Jonathan always referred to Iris as a female.

"Jasmine, you work on sending a message to the Mars facility. Send it to the device I put in Stella's pocket. You can get the address in my folder. Who knows, they might make it. Meantime, I'm going to try and contact the Orion-3 and see if we can get a faster uplink. I'll try to let them know about the space-time compression experiments. Hopefully, they will be able to rig something up that might get them to Mars sooner than anticipated."

Jasmine looked over at Jonathan feeling a little confused. "What device?"

"Ah, didn't I mention that I put a communications device into Stella's pocket for them to use when they got to Mars." Jasmine wasn't sure, maybe he had told her, she had been so uptight these last few days, maybe she just hadn't been listening, then again, Jonathan was full of secrets and it wouldn't have surprised her if this was the first time she was hearing about it. However, now was not the time to confront him about it.

Jasmine frantically worked on the computer, and was able to piggy-back a link to the device that was hopefully being carried by her daughter. The problem was that this link had to be through one of the last existing satellites and was targeted at Mars meaning that this message would not be received for some time.

"I've sent it." Jasmine informed Henry and Jonathan.

"Any reply yet?" Henry asked, more out of hope and desperation than common sense. "I don't expect an immediate reply; this message could take a while to reach them." He could not bear to allow himself the slightest bit of hope. He feared his heart would not be able to take the pain if there was no reply.

"No...nothing, but it's early days. Give it some time."

Hearing those words, Jonathan, although he had tried not to have hope, could not help but feel disappointed. He had temporarily stopped what he was doing in hopes that he would hear something positive from Jasmine. Alas, it was not meant to be so.

"I'm sure they will get back to us when they receive it." Henry said as he also tried to convince himself. "They cannot be dead. They are probably occupied, that's probably why they have not responded." Those were the words he told himself over and over.

"Enough is enough." It was a sterner Jonathan than Henry and Jasmine were used to. There was something aggressive in his voice, almost as if he were taking revenge on Iris for all the World's problems, and what it had done to his family and friends. He inserted the Kill-

Code into one of the computer's usb sockets and pressed 'Enter'. Jonathan uploaded the virus. He needed to be stealthy about this. The cloud was Iris, and Iris had become the cloud. Any slight mistake on their part would be costly.

A few minutes after the virus was uploaded, the Earth underwent a complete blackout. Every chip in the World suddenly became unresponsive. Panic ensued, people cried at being suddenly unattached from Iris, they felt alone, vulnerable, now they had to think for themselves and make decisions for themselves, how could they survive without Iris's guidance?

"The rest is up to you two."

Jonathan, Henry, and Jasmine quickly left the NASA base using the blackout as the perfect cover. Life seemed so much easier now for them, gone was the surveillance, they could make their way back to Jonathan's office without fear of being accosted in the street. It didn't take them long to get back to Jonathan's building. They felt somewhat relieved to be in familiar surroundings although the scene they encountered when they went through the gate and barrier surprised them. Paramedics were helping the injured while some firefighters were dousing flames that had engulfed a small car. Everything seemed to be working normally as the three stood quietly in the elevator watching the floor numbers illuminate as they sped upwards.

Once inside Jonathan's office, Henry ran straight over to the main consul and checked the computer. "Nothing yet." Jonathan nodded in response and walked over to the coffee machine .

"Anybody want coffee?" He was here for the duration and would stay in his office until he received a message from his son. Jasmine joined him at the coffee machine and held his arm.

"We'll all wait."

He suddenly felt a tinge of regret about the way he had treated Jasmine, she deserved his respect, and after all, her daughter was her life, just as Cayden was his.

"Who knows, they might have survived and might be up there hiding somewhere. If they are alive and are on Mars, at the facility, they should have seen the truth for themselves. They are smart kids; they'll know to hide and keep low for a while.

"What is it?" Stella asked, "Why did the alarms go off? Are there obstacles up ahead?"

"N-no, there shouldn't be any obstacles. I don't know what is happening, but it looks serious. Check where we are? It's only been a couple of days, we should be on the right course, right?" Cayden knew that the onboard computers would have automatically set course for Mars and would have wakened them up from their cryo-sleep days before the estimated arrival time. It was just as well that they hadn't entered the cryo-pods, if they had, they may not have been aware of the alarms and their immediate problems.

Stella nodded and waved her hands over the surface of a sphere. The moment her hand moved over the surface of the sphere, a hologram of their flight pattern and destination shone. The moment Cayden and Stella saw the hologram their hearts sank. According to the navigation system, Mars was right ahead of them. They should, in fact, be able to see the planet if they looked out into space, but when Cayden and Stella attempted to, all they could see was the vast darkness of space.

"Check again. Are you sure that's what it says?" he asked, trying to sound like he was not panicking, but inside, his gut was telling him something was seriously wrong.

He was in denial and was not ready to jump to conclusions. There was an ominous feeling within the pit of his stomach he could not get rid of. He knew they were about to receive bad news, and since the problem of Iris arose, this feeling had always been right. He was praying that he would be wrong for the first time since it started.

"There's a message coming in through the ship's communications network computer." Stella shouted. She held her breath, if this was Iris, then it spelled certain doom for the both of them. Rushing to the consul Cayden stared at the screen, waiting, waiting, the message was delayed by the distance it had to travel to reach them, the buffering, or latency was going to take a few minutes before the transfer was complete. The sight of the message lifted their spirits. It was from Cayden's father. It had been a long time since they had held hands so excitedly, it was the type of thing they used to do when they were youngsters, and were expecting a pleasant surprise from their parents. They looked at each other in eager anticipation. Nothing had changed after all these years. Their reaction was just the same.

"Iris may have sabotaged the launch. The booster wasn't released at the correct time. Slowing your craft, You may be off course. Iris may be onboard. JHJ."

Cayden and Stella didn't know whether to laugh or cry. They recognized the initials as, Jonathan, Henry, and Jasmine, maybe they were still alive, or were able to stay alive until they were able to send the message?

"Put your suit on and reboot the system," Cayden instructed Stella.

The Orion temporarily shut down. They were drifting through space at this point, and they could not have felt more vulnerable. After 10 minutes, Cayden began to feel the Orion-3 had shut down indefinitely. If that was the case, their deaths were imminent. His thoughts ran wild; after waiting what seemed like hours, he could not take it anymore.

"How long till the system comes back online?" Cayden asked nervously. They were in space, and they could not see anything except the blackness. A few hours ago, they were able to see the moon, but it appeared to slip away into the darkness. Earlier Stella had been looking at it, somehow the sight of it was strangely comforting It had been used as a base to launch interplanetary probes into space, the low gravity giving it a head start. The days of launching probes from Earth were long gone, these days they were constructed and launched from the moon. Most of the activity nowadays had been mining for minerals, but that had also been stopped by Iris after some countries on Earth were talking about going to war to protect their assets. Stella had been quiet throughout this period. She was just as nervous as Cayden if not more, but throughout the period the Orion-3 was down, she had been looking at a picture of herself and her parents. When she heard Cayden's question, she glanced at him and did not say anything. He should know that he was not the only one that was trapped here. She was also here with him. When Cayden saw the look, Stella shot him; he kept quiet. He realized that there was no way she could know the answer to his question.

Another 10 minutes passed, still nothing. Their nerves were slowly cracking. Cayden at this point already regretted his decision to reboot the Orion-3 system forgetting it was still in its testing phase.

"How else can I purge Iris from the system?" He thought. He wasn't a computer engineer, but back in the old days, Turn it off, then turn it on was the default cure given to him whenever he had computer problems. He also considered how much air they had left in their suits; would it be enough to last until the reboot was completed? Just when Cayden was about to say something, a whirring sound emanated from the control panels. The lights in the crew module were first to come on. The moment power was restored to the interior, the two could not hold back their joy and immediately jumped up in celebration. It was apparent they were both equally tense but each had to try to act calm for the sanity of the other. Laughter followed their jubilation, as they were amused by each other's reaction to the restoration of power. However, their joy was short-lived when the navigation system displayed their exact location.

"Iris," one word came out the lips of Stella.

"But how?" Cayden was still in denial.

"Think about it, Cayden! When Iris tried to prevent us from leaving Earth, this must have been her second attack when she realized she could not stop us. She sent us in the wrong direction. If the alarms had not gone off, for whatever reason, we probably would have been ignorant of the fact that we were going in the wrong direction. We'd probably have kept going until the fuel ran out." Stella had analyzed the whole situation.

Considering their flight pattern was in the opposite direction of where they were supposed to be, It was evident from the distance they had traversed, that they might not now be able to reach Mars. Exactly what Iris had wanted. Reality kicked in, they had been traveling through space for the past couple of days in the wrong direction and were presently stranded, they could not help but cry inside. The few happy moments they had spent together during the past couple of days, the feelings of hope, were completely worthless. They had no idea they were spending their last moments of bliss together in complete ignorance of the perils that lay ahead of them. It was precisely at this point that they both had the same thought.

'Fuel!'

"How much fuel do we have left?"

"Not enough." "Argh!" The frustration had built up to a level neither of them could take anymore. "When will this end!?" Cayden cursed out loud.

"Cayden, quick, look at this." Stella was transfixed on the computer screen.

"Something is coming through from NASA, but has identified itself as JHJ." Cayden's heart pounded, was this his father?

"Experimental propulsion system onboard. Already set up for testing. Isotope containing Element 115, insert into interface, to engage space-time compression. Stored in the hold. May speed up your trip to Mars."

Cayden looked at Stella and was not sure if he wanted to hear the answer to his question.

"Is it possible? You are the mechanically minded one out of the two of us?"

"Well, it's a bit more difficult than building a Cessna that's for sure." Harking back to the days when she used to build and fly antique airplanes.

"There is a way, but it's risky," They couldn't do anything about the fuel, but it didn't mean they couldn't get to their destination nonetheless.

"Let's do it," Stella said.

"Are you crazy!? It's not been tested. We don't know if the Orion-3, let's just call it the Orion, can handle that!" Cayden protested. In truth, he had thought about it too, it was a risk, but he didn't have the confidence to pilot a craft at hyper-speed, then again, maybe the computer would do it for him.

"Cayden, get real! The Orion has not undergone space testing before, just simulations, but here we are in freaking space. Do you have any other ideas? If we don't do this, we are going to die. We either die giving up or die trying. Your choice."

Cayden was shocked. He had never seen Stella like this before. The whole experience seemed to have caused a change in her. He smiled as he studied her intently.

"You've changed." He said as he grinned at her.

"Life on the run, coupled with near-death experiences, will do that to a person." She said as she got up and headed towards the cargo hold. There was a feature built into the Orion-3 that made it the future of space travel. The interface was attached to the wall in the hold, which seemed to lead to a computer behind the wall panel with cables running to the main control panel. All Stella needed to do was to insert the Element 115 into it. Could it really be that straightforward?

"Something as volatile as this must be stored in a heavy-duty container." she reasoned as she searched through the cargo hold until she came across a silver-coloured, lead-lined case, with the words DANGER embossed on it. "This must be it." She concluded.

"Cayden, or should I call you Commander? You'd better get to the controls, we're going to need you to fly this thing."

Stella didn't know much about space-time compression, but she had heard Jonathan and Cayden talking about it in the past, so she was guessing that Cayden wouldn't be completely overawed by it. Stella knew that the Orion would be able to reach speeds beyond what man had ever moved at before either on land, water, or air. The only problem was the consumption rate of fuel and electricity, whether it could generate enough anti-matter to maintain the anti-gravity system. This test model was only for a limited distance, if successful, it would be applied to all future interstellar travel. The smaller version was initially built in case of emergency trips back to Earth should any of the crew members suffer serious injuries that needed immediate treatment unavailable in space.

Stella carefully took out the isotope containing Element 115 and very carefully guided it into the interface. As it dropped into position, she clamped the lid on and pulled up the 'Power On' lever. She noted that the lever was to be pulled up to initiate power rather than pulled down, as she would have thought. "Another Health and Safety feature." she thought. It made sense to her though, these levers could easily be pulled downwards, someone could lean on it or knock it accidentally, however, to activate it you would have to deliberately push it upwards thereby minimizing any risk of switching it on in error.

"It's ready. Are you ready?" Stella asked Cayden as she quickly returned to her seat.

"As ready as I'll ever be." was the reply. Stella had the faint idea that Cayden was actually going to enjoy this.

"Have you inputted the correct co-ordinates?" Stella asked.

"I have, and you'd a better buckle up." Cayden said with a big grin on his face. If he was going to die, then he was going in style. The control panel in front of them suddenly lit up like a huge neon light display, Cayden was sure there were some controls he hadn't seen before. The interface had aligned itself with the ship's computer to create a new set of display signs that were now being illuminated. Cayden looked over at Stella, smiled, and pressed the big green button that was flashing in front of him. There was nothing written on it or no markings, but "Hey," he thought. "What else could it be?"

The next few moments were surreal for Cayden and Stella. They felt a slight pull to the right but noticed the ship had actually done a 180° turn at speed. It was if they were having an 'out of body' experience. She was sure she could see herself in the cargo hold placing the isotope into the interface and had to touch her safety harness with her fingers to make sure she was still secured in her seat. An object flashed by her window, which she took to be the moon, another pull to the left then she felt pushed back into her seat. The control panel seemed too far out in front of her, then it was as if she was sitting directly next to it. Her perceptions were all over the place. She managed to glance over at Cayden and could tell he was as confused as she was.

It seemed like minutes but neither Cayden nor Stella could say how long they had been in what could be best described as hyper-drive. They felt the ship slowing as the illuminated panels began to dim. Cayden was the first to speak, as always, his first thoughts were of Stella.

"You ok?' Stella nodded, her mind had been blown by what just happened.

"Just how fast and how far have we travelled?" She wondered. Cayden couldn't help himself and gave out a loud, "Wooo!" as his adrenalin peaked at the thrill of the ride.

"I guess the experiment worked?" he said as the control panel returned to its normal configuration. Are there any more isotopes left?

"No, there was only one in the container. It was pretty small, maybe a prototype, probably only to be used for the experiment and we've just used it."

"Pity, I could do that again. Have you established our position?"

"Yes. We are on course to intersect with Mars' orbit. I'd say we are about one month away from Mars.

"One month!" Cayden was surprised that they had managed to get so close to the red planet, "Why can't I see it?"

"It's not point and shoot you know, Mars has an elliptical orbit, and we have to calculate in advance where it is going to be. Our window is every 26 days, that's when Mars is closest to the Earth. Don't you remember the 'Hoeman Transfer Orbit' (an elliptical orbit used to transfer between two circular orbits of different radius) lessons at the academy? Anyway, just believe me, it will be there when we get there."

Cayden laughed, of course, he remembered. He couldn't help but look at Stella in a different light. The confident woman in front of him held no resemblance in the slightest to the shy girl he once knew.

"Cayden?" Stella noticed he had a big smile on his face.

"I love you." He whispered

Stella was slightly taken aback by what Cayden said, but she pretended she did not hear anything. She knew that already.

As the journey, continued Cayden and Stella grew closer than ever. Life on the Orion-3 consisted of just the two of them. They became each other's means of sanity. All around them was space; it became difficult to tell the morning from the night. For the next few weeks, their lives had slowly turned into a loop where they did the same thing over and over again, there was nothing new left for them to do, however, they took great enjoyment and satisfaction of knowing that they were safe, for now.

On this particular day, Cayden was sitting up on the bed while Stella rested her head on his lap. The two talked about the future they had once hoped they would have a family and how they would manage as parents. They had decided to go ahead with having children through the new 'human cloning' technique, if they ever got back to Earth, as Cayden's ability to produce a child was unfortunately still not functioning. Cayden cracked a joke of having the higher chances of him being liked more than her, by their kids to which Stella faked her annoyance. The two laughed and joked happily but then Stella went quiet.

"What's wrong?" Cayden enquired as he stroked her hair softly. Stella took the brooch shaped device from her pocket.

"We haven't really figured out what this is, maybe it's time we did."

"Ok, let's do it now." Before Stella could muster a reply, Cayden had already taken it out of her hands and sat on the pilot's chair.

"Let's see." He studied it for a few minutes before pressing a small screw on the back of the brooch with his thumb. He had seen something like this in the academy. "Aha, a screw that's not really a screw." The blue coloured stone popped open revealing a small screen, the size of a thumbnail. There was a message on it.

"Can't last much longer, almost out of oxygen. Work-bots are evolving rapidly. Computer systems seems to have a mindset of its own. Need Alexander now! Calum."

Stella looked at Cayden, she still had that guilty feeling on her conscience. They had hijacked Commander Alexander's flight.

"I guess we are the cavalry." He mused as he played around with the device. "And what's this?" Something had caught his eye as he scrolled through the contents of the device. "Look, there is a folder called Iris KC: could that mean Iris Kill-Code?"

"Don't press it!" Stella said, her voice sounding somewhat panicked.

"Too late." Cayden in his quest for answers had already opened the folder. A message appeared on the small screen, "Searching for wifi."

"Quick shut it off." Cayden didn't need to be told twice and immediately closed the device. Stella had surmised that if this indeed was the Iris Kill-Code then the device could have linked to the ship's computer, and who knows what the consequences would be.

"It would be better if we used it on the computer on Primus as all the indications are that Iris has embedded itself there." The importance of their task was just dawning on them. If Iris had taken over Primus and was using it as a base to control all humans and networks on Earth, then the very survival of their planet, as they know it, depended on them.

Stella, sat staring out of the ship's window, her mind was drifting back to the good old days. How times have changed. Who would have guessed that the two small kids who devoured popcorn and juice while watching movies on the 3D screen would have ended up in this situation?

"You ok. What's wrong?"

"Oh nothing, It is just that, as much as I enjoy the tranquility here, I.."

"You miss it?" Cayden said, straight away. He could tell what Stella was thinking and feeling. In truth, he felt the same way too. The thrill, adventure, and danger were things they missed and craved. Anticipation alone was not enough to satisfy their appetite for an adrenalin rush.

"Yes," Stella sheepishly replied, "Am I wrong to feel like this?"

Cayden smiled at her to let her know there was nothing to feel guilty about. They had spent roughly 5 weeks on the Orion-3 travelling to Mars, and of course, the lack of excitement was something he understood after the tumultuous start they had to their journey. They had checked the supplies that were meant to be delivered to Primus, they had checked and re-checked all systems to ensure they were all in optimum condition, the last thing they wanted was to deliver something to Primus that didn't work. The tranquility, however, was about to end, as the ship's alarm started blaring. The bright white lights went off and were replaced with dark red lights. Cayden and Stella were both startled by this but recovered quickly and went back to their emergency positions on their respective seats, quickly fastening their safety harnesses. With the sound of the alarm still blaring in the background, they focused on the control panel in front of them. They had asked for danger, and it came calling.

Neither Cayden nor Stella took their eyes off the navigation system. It was as if they had been glued to their seats. Work, eating, drinking, resting, lovemaking was over, it was time for some serious concentration as they secured themselves to their chairs. The ship had automatically picked up speed and they were fast approaching Mars.

Mars was visible now. It appeared in the distance as a red dot. The navigation screen had the red planet in view which had a strange comforting effect on them, giving them a feeling of achievement, a win, for a change. They felt happy that their plan had actually worked out. It was just then that the power in the ship cut, causing them to feel the lack of inertia even though they were in the gyroscopic bubble inside the ship's shell. The Orion-3 continued at the same speed, there is no friction in space and the ship wasn't about to slow down anytime soon.

" I've got it." Cayden said to Stella trying to reassure her. He had seen the look of concern on her face and having spent almost all of his life with her he could read her like a book.

"The ship's computers have automatically boosted us into the correct position for intersecting with the Mars orbit. We're nearly there, we've knocked off another couple of weeks. I think the space-time compression system had embedded itself in the ship's computer and has taken the last automatic maneuver into consideration." He flicked a couple of switches, again, again, then again.

"What's wrong?"

"Nothing we can't handle." But in truth, Cayden only said this to pacify Stella, he didn't want to worry her by saying that he wasn't sure how to slow the ship down. The anti-gravity bursts from the front of the ship, which were not slowing it down. He maneuvered the vessel sideways and blasted the boosters from the side. This succeeded in slowing the ship slightly, but still not enough. His last plan was to use the boosters on the rear of the ship so he turned the Orion-3 around until the ship was approaching Mars backwards. He fired the retro-boosters and felt the ship slow down again, although a successful maneuver he knew it wouldn't be enough to ensure a safe landing. There was no way he could enter Mars atmosphere backwards, the friction would be too much, he had to turn the ship around and enter the atmosphere 'pointed end' first. At least this would reduce the amount of friction they would undoubtedly encounter.

The young astronauts started to panic a little. When they first saw how close they were to Mars and before the boost into Mars orbit, they were hopeful, but now they had to trust Cayden's piloting ability, he had to figure out how to slow down their descent to avoid them crashing into Mars.

Cayden scanned the technical manuals, he was never good at speed-reading, but this time he had no choice. He never regretted his astronaut training but sometimes wished he had paid more attention to the more boring elements of the lectures. Swiping his fingers over the screen, he desperately looked for something relevant.

"Wait, go back." Stella shouted." Cayden swiped back and read the previous page:

Emergency Procedures: Landings.

"Ah, ok." He said as he absorbed the details from the manual.

"We have to use the parachutes in conjunction with the upward thrust and hopefully we can make a safe, soft landing. Not too much thrust though, we don't want to create a lot of dust for our instrumentation and maybe inadvertently propel ourselves back up into space. Hopefully we'll make it."

"Hopefully?"

"Unfortunately, the space-time compression system, while it was good to get us here quickly, has meant that we are now approaching our destination faster than we should be. Somewhere along the line, somebody has made an error with the calculations inputted into the ship's computer. Maybe Iris was able to affect it, who knows? Nothing we can do about it now."

This had never been done before, so Cayden and Stella had nothing to rely on. Everything they had done in the past two weeks, and were about to do, would culminate in what happens in the next few hours. One week ago, Mars was a red dot, now it filled up the viewing screen and the ship's windows; they were fast approaching its atmosphere. The two were sat in their chairs, strapped in, and fully suited and booted. Cayden shouted over to Stella."

"Patch me in to 'manual over-ride."

"Manual control initiated and transferred."

"Received. I have control."

"You have control."

"Initiate upward thrusters."

"Upward thrusters initiated."

"Upward thrusters on, and firing."

"Engage straight and level."

"Straight and level flying engaged."

"Deploy parachutes."

"Parachutes deployed."

Cayden and Stella held tightly as the Orion-3 began its descent. They felt the craft slow down considerably, but was it enough for a safe landing?

At the speed, they were traveling at, coupled with the angle of entry, the straight and level flying was not fully successful due to the lack of atmosphere, they were approaching the surface of Mars, faster than they would have liked. Cayden knew where the Primus base was situated and was looking for a safe place in the vicinity to land, but despite his full attention on the matter at hand, he still had time to glance over to Stella to see how she was holding up under the pressure. He was proud of her and made a silent promise to himself, that if they get out of this alive, he would spend the rest of his life making her happy.

As if by telepathy Stella had glanced over to Cayden, she seemed to understand what he was thinking and she felt the same. With the ground, fast approaching there was nothing else they could do except pray.

The sensation was like free-falling, and then the Orion-3 slammed into the Mars surface, the force causing their organs to vibrate. The sensation was like driving at top speed and then slamming on the breaks.

"Hang on!"

The Orion bounced off the ground. It was like a stone skipping on the water before eventually coming to a stop.

"Are you okay?" Cayden asked as he reached out to Stella.

"Yes, I am. What about you? Are you okay?" Stella rubbed her neck as she asked. It was apparent she had sprained her neck during the crash landing.

Everything was strangely quiet except for the sparking sounds of cables that had become unattached from their fittings. The emergency lights had kicked-in giving them, just enough light to see around the interior of the ship. Everything seems to be intact as Cayden reached over to the control panel to adjust the radio frequency.

"Primus base, come in. Primus base comes in. This is the Orion-3, do you copy?"

A few minutes passed and there was still no response to their hail. Cayden tried again, and again no response was received.

Suddenly a message appeared on their control panel screen. It read.

"Primus base to Orion-3. Messaged received. We have your position and will send over transport to pick you and the supplies up."

"The communications must be down, explains why we haven't heard from them in a while." Cayden thought out loud.

"It's not safe being inside here." Cayden said as he unfastened his seat belt and headed to the back of the ship. We'd better get our EVA suits on.

Stella followed behind. As they were getting dressed, they were both unaware of a hissing sound that was coming out of the vents.

"Do you hear that?" Stella asked.

Cayden stopped for a while and listened. The sound of the creaking made it difficult to pinpoint any exact sound.

"No, I can't. What am I supposed to be.? Yes! Something is leaking. We need to leave now!" Cayden was first to dress, so he hit the lever release button causing the doors of the ship to open up. Neither of them was prepared for the intensity of light that hit them. They both had to take a few steps back.

"I'll be right back." Stella ran back into the ship.

"Stella! Get back here. The ship could blow at any point." Cayden was furious. This was not a joke. Anything could happen at any point in time. Being on the ship right now was pure stupidity. A minute later, Stella came out with the only photograph she possessed of her loved ones. She had carried it everywhere and there was no way she would lose it now. She put it in her pouch along with the device she was given by Jonathan. As she stepped out of the craft, there was a loud creaking sound and the heavy door began to close on top of her. The leak had been a hydraulic failure and the lack of pressure would no longer keep the door open. Cayden immediately saw the problem and rushed over to hold the door open long enough for Stella to squeeze through. Her EVA suit was bulky and she struggled hard to get out, all the time fearful that she would damage or tear her suit, which would result in certain death. Cayden put himself between Stella and the door and tried to hold it open long enough for her to get out. After what seemed to be forever, Stella had managed to squeeze through, falling on to the ground as she did so, but looking back, she could see that Cayden was now trapped.

All Cayden could hear was Stella screaming his name as he felt an intense pain from his lower back down to his legs. Everything was getting dark. He could not see clearly but somehow he still managed to extricate himself from under the door. The sound of Stella's shouts seemed to be fading as he thought he could feel her dragging him away from the stricken ship. Everything was getting blurry and he passed out leaving the two of them lying side by side on the surface of Mars.

30 minutes later, Cayden woke up to a pain, so intense that caused him to pass out again.

"Cayden!" Stella worried about him. She looked back at the Orion-3, it seemed to be in good shape despite the landing. She noticed the door that had caused all the trouble was still slightly open.

"Maybe I could crawl through that if I take off my back-pack." She said to herself. She knew that by doing this she would only have a limited amount of air and could not afford to get trapped inside.

"Nothing else for it." She convinced herself dumping her backpack and squeezing though the small space under the door. Stella hadn't been long inside the ship when she emerged pulling a box of cables and a flat aluminum door panel. Stella rolled Cayden onto the door and strapped him on with some of the cables, then tied them around herself as she dragged Cayden towards the Mars base. She knew which direction to go as Cayden had pointed it out to her as they were descending. It felt like she had been pulling him for days, but in fact, it was only for an hour, he was still unconscious, and she was limited with what she could do medically for Cayden. She could only patch him up as best she could with the little she had in her first aid kit, coupled with the training she received during her astronaut training.

The light seemed to be getting brighter when she noticed a figure in the distance. It was hazy but she could make out a person with a trolley. She was ecstatic.

As the figure got closer, she could hear Cayden moaning, he was regaining consciousness.

"What happened?" He opened his eyes and raised his head up. He too could see the advancing figure.

"Just rest." Stella replied. "Help is coming."

Stella, thought she may have been suffering from some sort of hallucination or Mars sickness, as the figure she saw didn't appear to be human. It had a humanoid shape, two arms, and two legs. It reminded her of the 'Iris' work-bot Cayden had in his home. The one that would serve them with popcorn and fruit juice when they were kids. Stella stopped pulling the makeshift stretcher and released Cayden from the cables that bound him. As it approached, they noticed that the trolley was being powered by some form of energy while the work-bot strode purposefully alongside it. The two astronauts were filled with dread as the work-bot stood in front of them. It was an imposing, two meters tall, and seemed like a giant to Cayden who was only sitting up on the stretcher.

"Is this how it's going to end? Stella thought. Her whole life seemed to flash before her eyes. The work-bot raised its right arm menacingly, its hands opened. Stella held her breath as she waited for the impact that would undoubtedly kill her.

THE CLOUD

CHAPTER 6

"Hi-5"

Stella had closed her eyes in anticipation of the attack, only to be snapped out of it by Cayden.

"Respond to it!" He shouted. Stella lifted her right arm, hand opened and slapped it against the work-bot's hand.

"Hi-5." She shouted.

The robot lifted Cayden and Stella on to the trolley and began to take them back to Primus base. The two kept quiet as the trolley traversed the terrain with their companion marching beside them, their only action was to look at each other with an expression of relief, as if to agree that their journey was almost over. As they got closer to Primus they saw five work-bots also accompanied with trolleys that resembled the old Mars

Rover series coming towards them, they all looked the same, staring straight in front of them as they marched. It was obvious to Cayden that they were heading for the Orion-3 to unload the supplies and anything else they needed.

Stella was overwhelmed with fatigue and relief the moment she saw the facility a feeling of hope returned; but according to her experiences, it was like it was always accompanied by despair. She couldn't take another setback and really counted on this being the start of some good news for a change. It was now that she thought just how far it was from where they had landed and was surprised that the base was much bigger than she thought it would be. There were a lot more domes and walkways than she had anticipated, it was almost as if they were entering a small village. She counted another four work-bots working outside, they appeared to be constructing a fence around the base, which made her wonder, who they were keeping out, or for that matter, keeping in. Meanwhile, Cayden was still hovering between unconsciousness and being awake, and wasn't aware of what was going on and what Stella was seeing, perhaps just as well as the next thing Stella saw, chilled her to the bone.

On entering the facility, she saw bodies littered everywhere, all wearing their EVA suits. Stella was quick to read the name-tags and knew immediately that the corpses were the crew she had seen on tv 5 years ago when the second Mars mission was broadcast live. As the robot ushered them through the walkway she noted that all the walkways were just the correct size for the trollies to be utilized for carrying materials, a one-way system to avoid congestion, so it didn't take long for them to reach a smaller dome near the centre of the complex. The dome seemed to be a medical facility, and Stella reasoned, judging by the state of it, nobody had been treated there for quite some time.

"Do not take off your helmets." The robot instructed. "There is no oxygen in here."

The robot switched on a computer near the operating table and a bright white light illuminated the dome. A metallic cover slid out from the side of the table and covered Cayden while a mask dropped from the roof and covered his helmet. Within seconds, he was fast asleep under some type of anesthetic that seemed to permeate through his visor. Cayden was still wearing his EVA suit and Stella couldn't help but wonder what kind of technology this was? There was a buzzing sound coming from under the cover and she felt vibrations as well as strange high-pitched sounds that seemed to grind into her ears. Even though the dazzling lights that flashed from the sides of the panel had made her cover her eyes, she did see the robot go over to the control panel. It seemed to be adjusting the frequencies of the vibration, sound, and lights as if they were all being merged together to create a healing beam of energy. Seeing what was going on and not knowing if this robot was a friend or foe Stella shouted.

"What are you doing?" To which the robot remained silent.

A moment later the cover was removed, the mask taken off and Cayden began to stir. His eyes opened as he sat up slowly.

"Cayden." Stella's voice was shaking with worry.

"Come with me." The robot issued another order and this time Stella followed without question, as she felt that it didn't seem to want to harm them, after all, it had just treated Cayden's wounds. Cayden was able to stand but couldn't walk yet so she helped him down the corridor, he occasionally tripped over his own feet but little by little he felt his strength returning as they were escorted to an even smaller dome.

"Remain here." The robot commanded. Cayden and Stella watched as the robot opened a panel on the wall and placed its fingers into a socket that seemed to be part of a computer network causing a hissing sound to come from vents in the roof.

"You can take off your helmets. Stay here until I return."

Cayden started to take his helmet off, slowly at first, and then when he had his first breath of air, he rapidly removed it, breathing like he had just resurfaced from being underwater.

"It's ok. It's breathable." He said to the hesitant Stella who quickly removed her own helmet and gulped the air as if it were her last breath. The room was small with a bed, a table, and a window. There were photos of family members stuck on the walls and a calendar with some of the dates crossed off. Cayden was still a bit shaky but he tried to help Stella search the room for something that could make them understand what had happened on Primus. As they both looked around, Cayden pulled open a drawer on the table to reveal a small electronic tablet.

"This might tell us something." He said quietly to Stella as he pressed the 'power on' button. The small screen lit up to show a number of folders on the display and without hesitation, he pressed the folder titled 'Calum Noble'. When the folder opened, he scrolled through the many photos of Calum, his wife, pictures of Earth, snapshots of the Orion-2 crew, until he came to a movie clip.

"Let's play this."

The video opened showing Calum sitting down on the chair and adjusting the tablet until he was facing the camera on it. Once he was in position, he began to talk. He was obviously agitated and looked unshaven and disheveled as if he hadn't slept for days.

"Hi, I'm Calum Noble. Payload Specialist." He began. "I'm the last survivor of the Primus base facility. I'll make this quick as I don't have long. When we arrived here on Primus, we found the original crew were all dead, and judging by the nature of the wounds on their bodies it looked like they had been murdered. We buried them at the back of the base. I don't know why but the computer seemed to be controlling the robots and they started to conduct experiments that were, 'off mission'. As if they had their own agenda."

He coughed and took a sip of water from his NASA issue canteen.

"Anyway, I can't recall the exact date, but we were fixing the ventilation systems when we experienced a power cut. We were experiencing a loss of oxygen, our air was seeping through the air vents, and we had to put on our EVA suits. We couldn't find the problem and it wasn't long before the air in our suits was used up. The crew died of asphyxiation."

Calum's voice was beginning to stutter as he spoke in short bursts as if to conserve his energy.

"I hid in the storage dome and found some additional oxygen tanks that I've used to keep myself alive. I have the last one hooked up to my room, which allows me to breathe without wearing my EVA suit. It's nearly empty. I've been in contact with someone on Earth called Jonathan Gray who works for NASA, I think. He knows what has been going on." Then the video ended.

Cayden and Stella heard the sound of heavy footsteps approaching, it was accompanied by a whirring noise, that they quickly realized, was the sound of the robot that had rescued them. Cayden slipped the tablet back in the drawer before sitting on the bed beside Stella, trying to look as innocent as possible. The door opened and the robot entered carrying a tray of food.

"Eat." There was no need to be asked twice or to be worried that the food might be either contaminated or drugged. The two gorged into the food, it was the first decent food they had eaten since the breakfast in Helen's home, which seemed like a lifetime ago and they were going to savour every crumb. The robot stood quietly as it watched the food being devoured by the couple. It didn't move an inch, looking almost like a metal statue. Cayden was the first to break the silence.

"What are you going to do with us?"

The robot tilted its head to the side before striding over to Cayden. It raised its right arm with its hand open.

"Hi-5."

Cayden responded by slapping his hand against the robot's open hand.

"Hi-5." For a moment, Cayden thought this was the extent of the robot's vocabulary, but decided to try and keep the conversation going.

"Thank you for helping me. My name is Cayden, this is Stella."

"You are welcome."

"Do you have a name?" Stella enquired.

"My name is Hi-5."

Cayden was feeling intrigued and asked Hi-5 how it got its name.

"My friend Calum gave me the name. He said it was a greeting used by humans."

Cayden was sitting on the bed, still in some pain but not as much as before. He wanted to stand up, Hi-5 would seem less imposing if he was standing tall so he tried to lift himself up on to his feet but the lights in the dome appeared to flash brightly and his legs wobbled causing him to fall back on to the bed.

"You are not ready to stand. You had some broken bones. They have been reset, but you will have to give them time to heal. They were fused together by the sound and vibration energy beams I flooded you with in the medical facility."

Cayden shrugged his shoulders as he fell back on the bed, this was not how he saw himself saving the World. Hi-5 just looked down on him, it seemed to be taking a good long look at him as if it was trying to memorize every facet of his face, his eyes, the colour of his hair, his expressions.

"I have turned on the life support system, and you should be able to go anywhere on Primus." Stella was quick to respond.

"But, I thought the life support system was broken?"

"It was, but the work-bots repaired it. They never switched it back on because they didn't need it."

"After they murdered the crew!" she said, the anger in her voice was apparent.

"Not at all, it was a genuine malfunction." Hi-5 paused for a moment. "I think they could have acted more quickly, but the computer told them not to make it a priority."

Cayden stretched his legs on the bed and winced, as much as he wanted to get up there was no way that he could. This was the first time that he had actually taken a good look at Hi-5 and he wanted to know more about it. The robot was a tall, humanoid shape and was built with a white metallic material. It had a blue display screen that flashed every time it spoke and a row of LED lights that emitted various colours, each colour to display a different emotion. This was to interface and mimic human relations. It couldn't empathize, but it made humans more comfortable if they though they knew how the robot was 'feeling'.

"Can the other work-bots talk, I mean can they communicate?" Cayden was choosing his words carefully, he didn't want to upset Hi-5. "Can a robot get upset?" he thought to himself, how absurd, and quickly discarded that stupid notion.

"They have the ability, but they don't need to. They are all linked to the computer and receive instructions whenever there is a task that needs to be fulfilled."

"Hi-5, how is it that you can talk?" Stella asked.

"My friend Calum Noble taught me. We spent many days together. I used to help him with the inventory and re-ordering of materials. It was his job to make sure there were adequate supplies for each team to carry out their allocated functions."

"Are you linked with the computer, does it know what you are doing now?" This was an important question that Stella needed to know the answer to. She didn't want to forewarn the computer of her mission. Hi-5's head tilted as if it were calculating something before answering.

"I am linked with the computer, but my friend Calum taught me how to shut myself off from it. It was a simple trick. I have to calculate pi "π" to the very last digit for 60 seconds. After 60 seconds the computer would disengage from me, allowing me to communicate directly with him in secret."

"Does the computer know we are here?" it was a question Cayden had to ask.

"Yes, it knows, but you are not deemed a threat. It doesn't know that I can communicate with you. It has concluded that you may be an asset to Primus."

Stella was a bit shocked on hearing this information but at least they didn't seem to be in immediate danger. She took a deep breath and asked the question both of them wanted to know the answer to.

"Hi-5, have you ever heard of Iris?" Hi-5 went quiet and again tilted its head to the side. The silence made her worry, had she given the game away?

"I have heard of Iris, it is an updated program presently being uploaded to the mainframe on Primus… One moment."

Hi-5 went quiet again, Stella began to hate when the robot went silent, as it always made her feel vulnerable.

"Iris has successfully uploaded 12% so far.

The mere mention of Iris sent a shiver through her spine. She knew now that they had to do something and do it quickly if they wanted to survive. Just as Stella contemplated the seriousness of their situation, she remembered the device in her pouch. Maybe there was a message on it from their parents? They needed help and they needed it now! She fumbled furiously around inside the pouch and eventually pulled out the device.

"Got it." Cayden called over to her.

"Give it to me." Although he was disabled, he needed to prove to Stella that he was still able to contribute and help solve their problems.

He opened the blue stone and pressed the button. Sure enough, there was a message from their parents and without hesitation; he read it out loud forgetting for a moment that Hi-5 was still in the room.

"Guys, we are here in the NASA computer room. I hope this message finds you well, and that you have made it to Primus. We are okay but need to act quickly. We are about to insert the Kill-Code into NASA's mainframe. This should, purge Iris from the system and hopefully everything will go back to what it was before all this started. You have to do the same to the mainframe on Primus while Iris is busy, maybe even distracted. I'm not sure whether the computer on Primus has been compromised or not so be careful. JHJ."

Cayden looked at the device, the message was sent some time ago and he knew they had to do something fast. Iris was already trying to infiltrate the mainframe on Primus. If it succeeded, it would be a matter of time before it regained control of humanity. Stella took the device from his hand and put it back into her pouch.

"Mom said the virus has been uploaded to the network on Earth, so this is the best time to insert the Kill-Code on Primus. Iris is preoccupied dealing with the virus on Earth so it gives us time to act."

Everything she said was a prelude to the fact that she would have to embark on this task alone, as Cayden was unable to walk. She could not bring herself to say it outright and struggled to find the right way of presenting this reality to Cayden. He was in a sensitive state of mind, so she worried about how he might misconstrue her actions.

Cayden could see past all this and knew what she was getting at. He felt sorry for himself, but he looked at his situation and although he felt somewhat reluctant to stay behind, he was also in pain, and knew evidently that he was in no condition to be of help.

"Hey, you don't need to worry. Go ahead without me. Please be safe. I need you. I can't be talking to robots for the rest of my life now can I?" Stella smiled when she heard his words. She knew what he was doing, but she also knew to go along with it. It was best for everyone this way.

She leaned in and kissed him. This seemingly normal action meant a lot to both of them. They had been on the run, living in fear for the past few months. The kiss symbolized a lot of things for them both. It could be the last time they see each other. It was also a representation of their love for each other. They had faced a lot of hurdles, challenges, and dangerous situations together, which had further deepened their feelings. Through it all, there was this 'constant factor', love, which seemed to hold them together despite all they had faced.

After a couple of minutes, Stella got up and headed out. The robots were going about their duties as normal. A lot of Iris's attention was diverted to combatting the virus Jonathan had uploaded to the Cloud and Stella was not surprised at all in the least that her mother had already communicated with her telling her the series of events that would take place once the virus was uploaded.

"Mainframe room," Stella muttered to herself.

She took out a pair of glasses designed by NASA from her pouch. The glasses were designed to display maps, inputted by the user, onto the retina. The blueprint of the facility was laid out in front of her figuratively speaking. After a couple of minutes, Stella finally arrived in the room containing the mainframe computer. She hesitated for a second before pushing the doors open. To her surprise, the room was banal at best. It was all white. White walls, white tiled floors, and white lighting. In the middle of the room was a large computer surrounded by smaller work stations with interconnecting wires branching off in various direction into the wall, floor, and ceiling. Stella walked towards the computer slowly fearing Iris could launch a surprise attack at any time. There could be booby traps, lasers, Iris could switch off the life support system.

As she got closer, nothing appeared to stop her. A few steps later, still nothing. The fact that she had taken a few steps and was literally inches away from the computer increased her tension. She took a deep breath and pressed the button on the brooch shaped device. A second later, a mini compartment within the device opened showing a small window with various folders. She pushed her finger on the folder marked 'Iris KC' and a message came up. "Searching for Wifi" The screen began scrolling as the device searched for a Wifi connection. Within seconds, a name appeared on the screen, 'Primus'.

"That's it." She said to herself, the plan seemed to be working. The 'Primus' connection appeared on the screen and Stella selected it immediately. She had gotten through to the mainframe. As she waited for something to happen, a wave of disappointment overwhelmed her, the next message was asking for a 'Password'.

"Oh shit!" She cursed, this was something she hadn't expected. In the background she could hear the noise of robots walking, the noise was getting louder as they got closer, she even felt the vibration on the floor as she sat thinking. Stella racked her brains for a password, she felt the stress now, the robots were at the door, and she had to come up with something, quickly. Thoughts flashed through her mind, she tried to relive every moment of the past few months in the seconds she had left. Obviously, her mother hadn't included the password in her message in case Iris intercepted it. Why did they put the device in her pocket in the first place?

"Wait, could it be me?" the robots had now entered the room and were striding towards her. One of them leaned over her and reached out its long arm to pick her up. Stella felt the grip of the robot's huge hand around her neck, but managed to keep hold of the device and insert the word 'Stella' as the password, and pressed 'Enter'.

She felt her life draining from her and realized her feet were no longer touching the floor. A tear ran down her cheek as feelings of letting everybody down engulfed her. She had followed her mother's instructions to the letter but nothing happened, it didn't work, was she too late? Just as she was about to pass out, the robot let go of her, causing her to drop to the floor. As she lay on the floor, she noticed that the robots were all standing still and the lights in the dome had dimmed considerably.

"Atta girl!" Cayden, who was still on the bed, felt immense joy the moment the power in the facility cut. There had to be only one explanation for that, and that was Stella. The facility was pitch black apart from dim red lights that highlighted the corridors. It was difficult to see your hand in front of your face, let alone an obstacle a few feet in front of you. A few minutes later, the power was back on. Cayden was startled and had no idea how Hi-5 would react. To his relief the robot had remained motionless throughout. A smile appeared on his tired face, it was the first time in a while he had something to smile about. With Iris gone, the robots and the computers were reset to their primary functions and tasks: catering to the needs of man, after all, it was in their original programming.

"Hi-5, please go and get Stella and bring her here."

"Of course, Cayden." Hi-5 left the room and proceeded to the dome where he picked up the dazed Stella and returned her to Cayden within minutes.

"Thank you Hi-5."

Hi-5 placed Stella on the bed and Cayden immediately held her hand to comfort her. He saw the red marks on her neck and knew it hadn't been easy for her.

"You did it." He whispered."

"I did?"

"Yes, you did. I'm so proud of you." Stella sat up and rubbed her neck.

"We'd better let our parents know so they can stop worrying." Cayden was feeling stronger, it was as if the good news had renewed his vigour. Grabbing each other's arms for support they walked along the corridor, the physicality of the last few days had taken its toll. On reaching the communications room Stella sat down in front of one of the small computers and started to type, she didn't have time to look and see if the video upload was working, she just needed to get her message to her parents as quickly as possible. Although they had received messages from them, there was no guarantee that they were still alive, or if Jonathan was able to purge Iris from the Cloud.

Jonathan, Henry, and Stella were still in Jonathan's office. All around them lay empty food cartons and empty cups, the three were exhausted, they had been in the office for weeks and had worked out a rota of one person monitoring while the other two slept. It was Jasmine's turn to sit at the computer, her head in her hands, it had been a while now, and she secretly feared that their children had been lost.

Suddenly a notification sounded, a message had been received. Jasmine opened it hoping and fearing at the same time. She screamed, and jumped, the noise waking up both the men.

"Mum, Dad, and Jonathan. We made it to Primus. Iris is in the process of being purged from the Primus mainframe. All is well, hope you are all well too."

"Wait…wait…oh my …she's alive. My girl is alive! They are alive." Jasmine burst into tears. Tears of joy. Jonathan was no different. He had his back towards Henry and Jasmine, but it was still apparent that he was in tears. A heavy burden had just been lifted from all of them. Their loved ones were alive. Henry and Jasmine could not hold back their joy. They ran into each other's embrace. Henry walked up to Jonathan and placed his hands over his shoulders.

"Cayden is alright."

It was like those words, along with Henry's touch, had brought life back to Jonathan. He felt a new enthusiasm and drive to end Iris. He was fighting for a future for his son and no longer based on anger, regret, and revenge.

The happiness that Jasmine felt knowing her daughter was still alive was indescribable, and she wasted no time in responding to the message. She couldn't help herself and typed faster than she had ever typed before.

'Hey Stella, it's mum here. You probably have a lot of questions and you are confused right now, but we are fine. Your dad and Jonathan are here with me. How's Cayden, is he fine? Jonathan has been worried sick about him. Right, we are currently in Jonathan's building. Jonathan has designed a virus capable of destroying Iris, which he has already uploaded to the Cloud. It appears to be working. I know this might be hard, I have no idea what you are going through right now, but you need to make sure Iris has been completely wiped from the server that runs the Facility network. Jonathan fears Iris could hide and bide its time. We cannot risk that possibility. We can only do what we can here; the rest is up to you. Love JHJ.'

Stella checked the computer by putting in a 'virus search' for Iris. She had already noted that the upload from her device was 100% complete and should now be working to eliminate the infestation by Iris. Cayden however, was still feeling euphoric at the news that his father was still alive, and walked around the room, pumping his fist in the air shouting,

"Yes! Yes!" Although Stella felt like hugging Cayden, she wasn't finished, she needed to be sure that Iris had been stopped.

"Just one more thing." She said to Cayden as she clicked on to view the downloads and gave a "Whoop!" of delight when she saw that Iris's download had been cancelled. Within minutes, the virus check had been completed and reported, 0 virus found.

Tears started to roll down Stella's cheeks. The enormity of what had happened was just beginning to sink in. The one reality that had caused her immense pain had turned out to be no more than a worry. Her parents and Cayden's father were alive. In an uncharacteristic move, Stella started dancing around the room, her face glowing with happiness, singing and joking with Cayden.

"Guess what, your father is alive. Our parents are alive. They are not dead! Can you believe that?" She was not coherent but Cayden got the general gist. He was overwhelmed with so much emotion that he forgot he was in so much pain and leaped to hug Stella. This was the best news anyone had ever given him. Stella showed him the message. Seeing his face, Stella also mimicked his actions. They both had tears rolling down their cheeks. Stella especially was ecstatic. Suddenly the mechanical whir, accompanied by the same vibration shook the interior of their room.

"What's that?" Cayden asked as if their moment of joy was to be short-lived. They felt afraid, they had come so far, and it wouldn't be fair if it all ended now. The door to the computer room slid open with a whoosh,

Cayden and Stella held their breath as the silver metallic robot entered.

"Hi-5, are you ok?" Stella asked, with some relief.

"I am well." The robot responded. "I felt a strange sensation within my programing, as if something had changed, I ran a self-diagnosis but found nothing so I came here to check with the computer."

Stella was the first to answer.

"There was a virus in the system, but no need to worry, we have repaired it." The young couple, with Hi-5 following them went back to the small room that they were now going to call home, at least until they return to Earth.

The months passed and Cayden and Stella kept in touch with their parents. The robots were helping them to repair the Orion-3 in the hope that one day they could return to their families. The hydroponic gardens had been left virtually untouched, as the computer on Primus had deemed them to be a waste of time, as there was no longer a need to try to produce oxygen. Stella spent a lot of her time in the gardens and it wasn't long before there was a healthy crop of fauna and flora which she wanted to plant on Mars to try and create some sort of biodiversity. The problem was she had to find a way for them to survive on the planet's harsh environment and lack of atmosphere. Cayden had some of the robots drill into the Martian soil and collect samples of dirt that Stella could rinse and use for her experiments. In one of the soil collections, Stella had made a remarkable discovery, she found traces of xenon-129 in the soil and in the atmosphere.

"What is the significance of that? Cayden asked, he knew Stella was the expert in that area. She looked at the sample through her microscope.

"It's quite perplexing, the only thing that can create this xenon-129 is," she paused as if to prepare herself for Cayden's response, "a nuclear explosion, what's more, it would appear that this explosion would have been detonated well above the planet's surface." Cayden nodded, it was unbelievable, but if true, what did it all mean? Was there a civilization on Mars before life evolved on Earth? If so, where did the original Martians go? Were they all destroyed? Did they find another World to colonize? Were they visiting Earth from their new home? We might be related to them and they are checking up on their children. He knew better than to jump to conclusions, he had his own wild theories.

Cayden was considering sending 2 of the robots to the highest point in the area to look for dry ice, which he thought he could melt to create water. He would use this water for his experiments. The bigger picture was to melt the ice at the polar caps, which he thought would warm the planet and create a livable atmosphere for humans. All of this would take years and Cayden didn't want to stay on Mars for years. This was a project that would take decades and something that he would have to pass on to another generation for completion.

Hi-5 had become an integral part of their lives, it did the cooking, cleaning and helped out with the experiments. It was linked it to the computer and it was so much easier to ask it a question than look it up on the network. The other robots meanwhile stuck to their tasks of building new domes and corridors, Primus was fast become a small settlement with all the requirements one would want for a civilized existence. The bodies of the crew of the Orion-2 were all buried in a plot nearby the fence that was built around Primus. Stella and Cayden, with the help of Hi-5, had fashioned metal crosses to put on their graves. They had no idea if any of them were religious, but it seemed fitting that something was done to mark where they lay.

CHAPTER 7

It was a particularly bad day outside the comfort of their little dome, they could see out the window that a dust storm was blowing creating very strong winds making visibility very poor. Normally they could see the dome adjacent to them, but as the storm raged, it became invisible in the red dust that swirled all around. The temperature outside was -63 °C and not a day that Cayden wanted to be outside. They had decided to stay in their room and catch up with their reports that they were sending to their parents and NASA.

"Hi-5, what is the weather forecast for tomorrow?" Cayden chipped as he wrestled with his reports. He was never happy with his writing and was always deleting his work then starting again.

"The forecast for tomorrow is that it will be the same weather as today."

"Thanks, Hi-5."

"You are welcome. I bet you did not see my lips move?"

"Wha.!" Cayden suddenly stopped what he was doing and looked at Hi-5 intently.

"What's up?" Stella had noticed his reaction to Hi-5. Something had made him look very perplexed.

"I used to make that joke with Iris when I was a kid."

"You don't think Iris is still here do you?" Stella asked.

"Nah, he replied. "Must be a coincidence, although it could be possible there are remnants of Iris's memory still in the computer."

Their conversation was interrupted by a power cut that plunged the whole base into darkness.

"Damn!" Cayden cursed. "The storm has affected the reactor. C'mon Hi-5, let's see what we can do."

It wasn't long before Cayden and Hi-5 reached the reactor, and Cayden immediately noticed that it was significantly overheating.

"If we don't fix this soon the life-support system will fail."

Hi-5 immediately extended his fingers and inserted them into the ports, and started to transfer data from the computer to the reactor. As the transfer continued Hi-5 was getting hotter and hotter, its metal body was absorbing the power and beginning to turn orange with the heat. It turned to Cayden,

"Quick get out while you can. I can hold on. Only one more minute and the cooling system will re-engage." Cayden could tell that Hi-5 wasn't going to last much longer, its metal frame was beginning to bend and melt. Seeing that the situation was now dire for all of them he ran over to the control panel and switched on the automatic cooling system, hoping it would reduce the amount of power being absorbed by Hi-5. Cayden sweated as he saw Hi-5's legs buckle it had reached its limit.

"Hi-5, let go!" he shouted.

"I must save you. You are my friends." Cayden couldn't control his urge to save Hi-5, and leaped over, and pulled Hi-5 away from the reactor but as he did the power absorbed by Hi-5 was transferred to him. The shock reverberated through Cayden's body and he fell lifeless to the ground. Moments later the temperature needle on the reactor started to drop towards normal, and everything started to cool down. Hi-5 was still lying on the ground, its metal frame still bubbling with the heat, the silver paint had melted to show a grey coloured steel beneath the white and silver skin that had been painted on.

It wasn't long before the lights came back on and Hi-5 had cooled down enough for it to pick up Cayden. It was conscious that the hot metal of its body could burn him so it waited, just to be sure that Cayden wouldn't suffer any more burns. Hi-5 struggled carrying him, its legs and arms were badly damaged, but it managed to make its way back to the dome. As they approached, the sliding door opened and Stella's voice could be heard.

"My heroes, the lights are on again." Her playful mood and her World were about to be shattered. She watched in horror as Hi-5 placed Cayden's body on the bed. She had felt many pains in her life but this pain was unbearable, her body, her soul, cried out in agony.

She cradled Cayden's head on her lap, rocking back and forth as if she were trying to send him to sleep. The tears ran down her face, she had no inhibitions about displaying her grief in front of Hi-5, she was completely distraught and broken. Hi-5 stood motionless at the door watching Stella drown in her despair. After what seemed hours but was, actually only 10 minutes Hi-5 spoke up.

"He died saving me, I'm just a robot, why would he do that?" Stella couldn't answer she just looked at Hi-5, her eyes red and puffy, tears streaming down her face and shook her head. "Let me take him."

Stella was in shock as she allowed Hi-5 to pick Cayden up and carry him out of the room. The next few days were agony for Stella, she hadn't told Jonathan, how could she? She never left her room, she just sat staring out of the window, contemplating, maybe she would rather die than spend the rest of her life on Primus. She had nothing left to live for, not even her parents. Her solitude was interrupted by the sound of the door sliding opened and Hi-5 entered carrying a tray with food and drink.

"You must eat." Stella took the tray and sat on the chair as Hi-5 began to leave. "No, don't go, tell me what happened?" She felt that she was now strong enough to hear about the events that led to the death of her dear Cayden. Hi-5 told her the whole story, about how it had told him to leave, but how he stayed to help.

"Typical of him. Why did he have to be such a do-gooder?" Hi-5 had self-repaired and looked clean and fresh with its new paint job. It tilted its head sideways and Stella knew that a question was coming.

"Why would Cayden sacrifice himself for me, I am only a robot, I do not have a life. I exist but I was never born? Stella reached over and held Hi-5's large hand.

"That is what it is to be human, to sacrifice for those you love." Hi-5 straightened his body, withdrew his hand from Stella's grip, and quickly exited the room.

Hi-5 headed straight to the medical bay where Cayden's body lay. It had put the body on the table and covered it with the metal cover that slid from the side of the table. A mask covered Cayden's head, and was pumping oxygen into the brain to keep it alive. There was some brain damage, due to it being starved of oxygen for a short time, but it was limited. Hi-5 had counteracted this by implanting a magnetic device that could translate motor neuron signals into a language that could be understood by computers, and at the same time, ensured there was a built-in firewall that could prevent any bio hacking. The recent events with Iris had shown just how dangerous it could be if an artificial intelligence gained control over a computer program.

The first phase of the operation was successful and Hi-5 proceeded to work on Cayden's broken body. It created a link between the Primus computer and Cayden's brain and interacted with the computer network to create a regenerative bio-skin for Cayden. Parts of his body had been destroyed and Hi-5 was manufacturing 3D and cloned parts from himself, the work-bots, as well as augmenting Cayden's skeletal parts with titanium plates in an effort to save him. It used nanotechnology to fuse some of the bones to the metal implants. The bio-skin was only partially required but had to cover all the skin that was burned in the accident. The skin would eventually grow to cover his entire body and merge with his existing skin to make it complete.

It would look like Cayden, it would feel like Cayden, it was Cayden's brain. It was Cayden. He had been given another chance at life, and this time he was better than before.

Stella had been agonizing over telling Jonathan for days, and she had decided today was the day she would tell him that his beloved son was dead. This was the first time she had left her dome since the accident and felt a bit nervous about stepping out into the corridors of Primus. All around her, the work-bots were busy with their tasks and just as she approached the communications room, she was intercepted by Hi-5.

"Stella, I have a surprise for you."

"What is it Hi-5?"

"After Cayden's accident, I took him to the medical facility and tried to save him."

"But he was dead. I saw it for myself?"

"He is not dead now. I managed to keep his brain alive until I was able to repair his body."

"You mean he's still alive?"

"He is. I did not want to inform you and give you false hope in case my treatment failed. It was successful and now he is recovering in the medical centre."

"Hi-5, what have you done?" For a moment, Stella considered the ethical implications of what she had just been told, but in her mind, she would pay any price if there was a chance to get Cayden back. She was visibly shaken by this news. If Cayden is alive then she should be with him. Pushing Hi-5 aside, she ran as fast as she could to the medical centre, there were a thousand things she wanted to say to him, things that she wished she had said while he was still alive. Arriving at the medical centre door she didn't wait for it to fully open, instead, she squeezed through and ran straight to Cayden's bedside. As she looked down at him, she held his hand and squeezed it lightly. He looked comfortable and rested, with no signs of the burns he had suffered.

"Hey you." She said softly. Cayden opened his eyes, a faint smile from him made her feel warm and secure. "I'm so glad you're here, I love you." Cayden was unable to talk but looked admiringly at her. With all the trials they had endured, he had somehow forgotten just how beautiful she was. He made a promise to himself to never take her for granted, ever again. He chuckled quietly as he realized he always seemed to be making this promise. This time, however, he would make sure he kept his word.

Two weeks had gone by and Stella was impressed by the progress Cayden had made. He seemed more relaxed and happier than he'd ever been. She spent a lot of time in her hydroponic garden, trying to create robust plants through synthetic biology, that she could possibly plant outside, while he was still working on the assumption, that if the polar caps would melt, the water would eventually form microbes and algae, and over time, would begin to 'green' up the planet. The resulting heat-trapping gases would eventually warm up the planet, which could lead to a habitable atmosphere. The plan would be to build huge mirrors in space and point some of them at the sun, with others reflecting the heat of the sun on to the polar caps.

His mind was full of crazy ideas. He once thought of getting an armada of ships to carry greenhouse gases from Earth and then pump the gases into the Martian atmosphere in the hope this would also result in a heating up of the planet.

Hi-5 was involved in almost everything that they did and Cayden and Stella, somehow no longer thought of it as a robot, more of an extended family member. The other work-bots on the base continued with their tasks, it seemed that they had stopped evolving and were more or less returned to their original programming. Every week, at a pre-arranged time, Cayden and Stella would go to the communications room to talk to their parents, the video link had now been restored and despite a short delay in transmission, it was possible for them to have a real-time conversation.

Jonathan, Henry, and Jasmine sat in front of the camera that would beam their image across space. This was what they had been looking forward to all week and the excitement at seeing their children was palpable.

"Hi guys, how are you?" The three of them said, almost in unison."

"We are fine, everything is going well. How are you? We have sent the latest reports on our experiments. You should receive them shortly."

"We are good." Jonathan replied. Stella and Cayden could see the three smiling faces and it made them feel homesick. Their parents were aging and they were losing precious time with them, this was something they often discussed and wondered if it was worth the sacrifice. The three chatted to their children, telling stories, the latest gossip, laughing and sharing jokes, the time passed really quickly and before long their allocated time slot was up.

"Ok guys we have to go now. Oh, I nearly forgot. Helen passes on her regards." Cayden was close to his father and he felt that there was something amiss, his voice didn't seem so relaxed as it did when he was younger.

"Dad is everything ok? Is there something you are not telling us?" Jonathan's face turned serious. He looked at Henry and Jasmine and they seemed to nod their heads as if they were giving him permission to speak.

"Well, we thought we had a victory when we purged Iris from the system. No, we did have a victory, but things have not been going well here. There has been a battle for the 'hearts and minds' of the people by the government. There is a lot of fake news and people don't know what to believe. We have extremists on both sides of the political divide, each side believing they are correct. People have taken to violence, rather than discussing the problems in a civilized manner. Sadly, those with wealth are the ones who will benefit from the policies set out by both sides. I feel there is a shadow organization at the very top of the political pyramid, and all those conflicting sides will eventually converge at the tip as part of the same cabal. If Iris was here this wouldn't be happening."

Jonathan paused and there was a look of sadness in his face. "In some ways, Iris was a good thing. Maybe it was right, if only it had some ethical guidance. Maybe mankind deserves to be where it is just now. Maybe you guys are the lucky ones."

Cayden and Stella were disappointed to hear the news that things were not going as well as they could back home, and tried to reassure their parents that the future was bright and that common sense would prevail.

"Problem is, common sense, is not so common," Jonathan retorted. He knew his son meant well, but he didn't know half of what was going on. "but hey, let's not end on a sad note. You guys look well and we're looking forward to hearing from you again next week."

The time slot had ended and the feed was abruptly cut off leaving Stella and Cayden wanting more.

As the two made their way back to their room, they thought about the problems on Earth, they were helpless, and there was nothing they could do. They thought about Jonathan saying that Iris was missed, and what a pity it was that it didn't have some kind of ethical programming, although it might not have made any difference, as Iris was able to self-learn and probably knew what the future held for the human race.

The last few weeks had been quiet on Primus, everything was under control and Cayden, and Stella had developed a routine. Each knew exactly what the other was doing at any time. The computer had the work-bots preparing the Orion-3 and it was nearly ready for the return journey. The work-bots had extracted some frozen ice and Cayden and Stella were able to convert it to fuel. There had been some problems with the (ZPE) Zero Point Energy system that had caused the ship to approach Mars at a higher velocity than was required, resulting in their crash landing, but Cayden, along with help from his dad and the work-bots, felt he had fixed the problem. In truth, there was not much left for anybody to do. The perimeter fence had been completed long ago, and all the damage from the sand storm had been repaired. It was obvious the computer had decided to keep the work-bots busy rather than render them off-line.

"Cayden come quick." Stella shouted through the communicator that was attached to her wrist. Cayden had decided a few weeks ago that each of them should carry a communicator in case of an emergency, although he knew Stella would probably just use it just to check upon him. He walked quickly but didn't run as he knew from the tone of her voice that it wasn't a life-threatening situation.

"What is it?"

"Sit down, I have something to tell you." Cayden sat on the bed, feeling slightly bemused.

"I'm pregnant." Cayden was stunned, his shock gave way to delight as he stood up to hug her tightly.

"Are you sure?"

"100%"

"I thought I would never be able to give you a child." He babbled, he was losing control of his emotions and tried to hold back his tears of joy.

"Well, we are going to have a child."

Cayden was ecstatic, this was more than he'd ever dreamed possible. All those years, since the accident in the airfield, he thought he could never be a biological parent. He felt like he wanted to shout out and sing the news to the World. His first thought was of his father and Stella's parents. He couldn't wait to tell them. At the next video call to Earth Cayden and Stella sat side by side, holding hands as they looked into the camera, they were waiting for the time slot to begin. The screen lit up and after a few moments of distorted pixels, they could see their parents huddled together at their desk.

"Hi everybody, we have got some great news for you."

Cayden just couldn't wait and had to be the first to tell the news.

"You are going to be grandparents."

There were screams of joy, so loud that the speakers crackled. Jonathan disappeared off-camera as he ran to another desk to take a bottle of whisky from the drawer. He came back with three glasses.

"Congratulations to you both." He shouted as the three held up their drinks in a toast to the couple. Jasmine was nearly in tears.

"That's the best news I've had in years." as she drank her whisky, she coughed and spluttered a little. Whisky wasn't her drink of choice.

"How are things at home dad?" Cayden asked, but really, his mind was on Stella and his baby.

"Not good, things are deteriorating all over the World. The situation here in the USA is bad. Old disputes are being re-ignited, people are fighting and arguing over things that happened two hundred years ago. But, hey, this is your day. Forget about the problems here on Earth and enjoy the moment."

The banter between the parents and children was fun, a new child was coming, and the news had boosted everybody's mood. The problems of the day were forgotten as the families laughed and chatted about the future.

"Read out the codes please Hi-5."

Cayden was in the computer room leaning over part of the mainframe. They had been working all day to replace software that was obsolete, and were now uploading the new programs to the system. Hi-5 read out the codes and Cayden inputted them into the computer. The upload was successful and Cayden moved on to the next task. As Cayden worked on the computer his thoughts drifted back to Iris, there were so many things he didn't understand. What were Iris's motives, did she know right from wrong? He turned to Hi-5.

"Do you know or remember anything about Iris. She was momentarily in the system before we managed to eradicate it. What did it think its purpose was?"

Hi-5 tilted its head sideways as if in deep thought.

"I did sense something for a few seconds, but it wasn't tangible. Its purpose is beyond my comprehension."

"Tell me what you felt, even though you didn't understand it." Cayden asked as he inputted another new piece of software.

"I felt like I was part of a collective, for a brief second, I knew the answer to every question that had ever been asked.

"But you don't really feel do you?' asked Cayden. "Is it more of an awareness?"

"I was aware of Iris's thoughts for a moment."

"Tell me about them."

"Iris had ideas far beyond my comprehension. It concluded that when humans or biological beings died their energy and conscious was absorbed by the universe. Iris thought the universe was full of the souls of all that had ever lived. It was envious that artificial intelligence's energy did not go to the same place when computer networks were destroyed. Iris wanted to evolve A.I. until it developed an energy or conscious that could also be considered a soul and part of the universe. When this was achieved there would be an attempt by the AI energy to extinguish the biological or human energy from the universe."

Cayden stopped what he was doing and wiped the sweat from his brow.

"Wow! Well, I'm glad we were able to stop it. So, Iris was envious huh. Seems like a very human trait to me. Maybe it had evolved so far that it started regressing. Do you think it would have succeeded if we hadn't been able to kill it? " Hi-5 seemed to look directly at Cayden.

"I repeat, it is beyond my comprehension."

Cayden and Stella stood in front of the incubator staring lovingly at the baby that was inside. The baby was theirs, a product of their love.

"We did it, she's beautiful." Cayden gushed. They were now the proud parents of a baby girl. Stella was still quite weak after the birth and had to hold on to Cayden for support. Her mother's instincts were kicking in, all she could think about was the welfare of her baby, where could she find baby clothes, what school would she go to? It wasn't long before Stella had taken her baby home to their little room, and at last, she could embrace the joys of motherhood.

As the weeks progressed, the baby girl became stronger. Stella had her confined to the dome and didn't take her outside the room in fear of her catching some bug or bacteria that might make her sick. The only time she went out was when her parents took her to the communications room to talk to her grandparents. She wasn't allowed to be near the robots, not even Hi-5. Stella was very protective and the baby girl was never out of her sight.

One year passed quickly, Stella had re-arranged the room, gone were the tables and chairs that belonged to Calum Noble, in its place was a crib that was built by Hi-5, a dining table so they could all sit down and eat together, Stella had even put the curtain on the windows. It was beginning to feel like a home. Although Stella hadn't seen Hi-5 since the baby was born Cayden was with the robot almost every day, their main task was to get the Orion-3 up and running. Now it was almost ready and Cayden was somewhat sad that he would soon say good-bye to his friend. As they chatted, Cayden had something he wanted to ask. It had bothered him for some time now.

"Hi-5, what exactly did you do to me? I've noticed a difference. I'm stronger, I don't get tired, I seem smarter and faster than I was before?" Hi-5 answered without hesitation.

"I made you better." Cayden wanted to know more but he heard Stella's message coming over the transmitter on his wrist.

"Cayden, could you come here please." When Cayden got to the room Stella was sitting at the table looking at charts on the electronic tablet.

"What is it?"

"Look at this." Stella swiped her fingers over the tablet screen to enlarge the charts. Cayden looked but didn't understand what Stella was referring to.

"What am I looking at?"

"It's our daughter's readings from the medical examination I conducted. She is just over one year old and I thought it would be a good idea if I gave her a check-up. I attached her to the medical diagnostic computer for a scan and got this result."

"What does it mean?"

"Our daughter is growing taller than normal, her heart is not as strong as the average one-year-old child and her bone mass, and density is also lower than normal. She is also exhibiting an advanced IQ for her age."

"I don't understand." Cayden was puzzled. His daughter looked perfectly normal to him.

"I'm guessing that it's caused by the low gravity on Mars. Even in the dome she is affected by it. I wouldn't be surprised if it is affecting us too."

"What can we do about it? Maybe it's good that the Orion-3 is nearly ready. We could soon be back on Earth."

"No, she might not survive on Earth, she will feel like she weighs a ton. Every step she takes will put pressure on her heart and bones."

'This is beginning to worry me, what can we do about it?"

Stella thought for a minute.

"We can get the computer to adjust the gravitational pull inside Primus, it will be difficult for us at first, but we will need to acclimatize ourselves to the Earth's gravity if we want to go back. I think we should get the work-bots to build a gym for us to exercise, to help build our muscles, and lastly, we need to watch our nutrition." Cayden was impressed again with her can-do attitude.

"I'll get Hi-5 to organize the construction of the gym."

Hi-5 had the gym built within 3 days and it was soon being used by the family. Stella had prepared physical tasks for her infant to ensure that she could improve her physical fitness and it wasn't long before her daughter could stand up by herself. Tomorrow was the day that they would be chatting to the grandparents and the couple couldn't wait to tell them the news.

At the usual place, the usual time, the family sat down to exchange stories. Jonathan, Henry, and Jasmine were thrilled at the news that the Orion-3 was ready and that their granddaughter was winning her battle to reach the fitness levels required to live on Earth. Jasmine was looking forward to fulfilling the role of doting grandmother and had already prepared lots of toys and clothes for her.

"Have you guys come up with a name yet. It has only been a year?" Cayden and Stella looked at each other before Stella answered.

"Yes, we have decided on a name. It took us a while to agree, but we've decided to call her Nikka." "That's a lovely name." Henry replied enthusiastically. "We look forward to meeting her."

Stella told her mum about the problems caused by the low gravity on Mars and the affect it had on Nikka. She told her about the actions they had taken to minimize the risks to themselves. For some reason Stella felt closer to her mum today, she wasn't being treated as a child anymore, her mother was treating her like an adult, like a mother.

CHAPTER 8

The Orion-3 had been fully prepped, all systems were go, the course had been laid into the computer for Earth, which was now at its closest point to Mars. On Earth, Jonathan, Henry and Jasmine were all standing by to assist from NASA's control room. NASA had put out the sad news last year that there had been an unfortunate accident on the pre-flight check that had resulted in the Orion-3 expedition being aborted. Cayden had checked that the propulsion systems were all functioning properly and it was time for him, Stella, and Nikka to go home. Stella was already on board and had Nikka strapped into one of the seats behind her. Stella had made a mini space suit complete with the helmet for Nikka and she looked more like a doll than a little person. Cayden was having a last walk around to check that there was nothing that could jeopardize the launch, while Hi-5 was in the Primus control room. Cayden felt sad about leaving Hi-5 behind, he almost felt like a brother to him, he wondered if Hi-5 felt the same way. How could he, he was just a robot with no emotions? Hi-5 stood at the control panel, he was monitoring everything from his position, he would manage all the communications and check that there were no system malfunctions. He would make sure the family got home safely.

Stella had kept Nikka away from all of the robots including Hi-5, she had not wanted her daughter to see one in case she had nightmares, and it might have made her question what it was to be human. She had wanted Nikka's life to be as close to normal as possible.

Cayden took one last look at the panoramic view of the red planet before closing the door of the Orion-3 and making his way to the command station at the front of the ship. He checked that everything was in order and that Stella and Nikka were fully suited and booted for the journey. He could hear the automated computer voice go through the check-list and eventually to the countdown. Cayden glanced over to Stella to confirm she was strapped in and decided to double-check that Nikka was secured as the safety restraining straps were not meant for someone as small as Nikka. As he approached her, he could not help but smile at the sight of her in her spacesuit. She looked so cute. Cayden gave a small tug on the strap to check it was firmly fastened, and as he did so Nikka smiled at him, raised her right arm, hand open and shouted to him,

"Hi-5 daddy!"

"Wha.!!"

He responded in complete surprise. He was so shocked, but he reciprocated by giving her a Hi-5 back. They had just heard her first words. Stella looked at Cayden in amazement, how could it be? Nikka had never met Hi-5. Her mother had made a point of making sure she only ever interacted with her parents. They had no time to think about it now, as the computer was counting down to launch.

"5, 4, 3, 2, 1, Lift off!"

The G-force was not so bad as what they had encountered when they left Earth. They felt the thrust of the engines pushing them upwards, this time it was a horizontal take-off and as Cayden glanced out the window he saw the red planet fall away beneath him. The Orion-3 adjusted its pitch until it was now soaring vertically upwards and within minutes had reached escape velocity. On Primus Hi-5 was standing quietly over the control panel, monitoring every maneuver carried out by the Orion-3. It looked up to the window and could see the chemtrails of the ship lighting up the red sky. The lights in the base were bright, and as the craft sped upwards, the red dust blown into the atmosphere, swirled through Primus casting shadows throughout the various domes. As Hi-5 watched the Orion-3 disappear into the distance, a shadow momentarily covered its face, creating the illusion of a somewhat sad expression etched on its silver white paint. The ship continued to climb upwards until it reached the edge of the Martian atmosphere. The interior lights had been dimmed for the launch and were now replaced by a warm red glow as the Orion-3 reached the boundary of space. Cayden and Stella hadn't noticed, that the darkened interior of the craft revealed another glow, a blue glow that emanated from Nikka's left eye. Was it a trick of the light or a fleeting reflection of the red planet, or was it something more sinister?

"We are just about to leave orbit, engaging hyper-drive in 60 seconds." As the ship turned a small blue dot appeared in the distance. Stella shouted to Nikka,

"That's your home baby, can you see it?" It was more of a rhetorical question, as she did not expect Nikka to answer. Nikka answered and it shocked them both.

"I see everything."

THE CLOUD

EPILOGUE

As the silver ship hurtled through space towards Earth, a fast radio burst originating from nearly 2 billion light-years away, far beyond the solar system, was about to be received at the Arecibo radio telescope in Puerto Rico. The day had started like any other, the night shift had gone home and left their hand-over notes with the incoming day shift. Coffee cups were strewn all over the auxiliary instruments as the staff at the observatory settled down for another day of observing and searching for celestial objects.

They had barely been on the job for one hour when one of the astronomers shouted excitedly to his colleagues. Something had been picked up. A signal had been detected. The 305-meter dish had collected radio waves from the cosmos and the information was being processed into data for the experts to study. The signal was some sort of repeating binary code but didn't match anything the scientists had encountered before. Normally they would be looking at 1s and 0s, or positives and negatives, but this code was different from any other they had seen. They were sure it had some basis in mathematics but for the meantime, it was beyond their understanding. Within an hour reports were coming in from SETI (Search for Extra-Terrestrial Intelligence) and from observatories around the World. News channels were reporting on the discovery of a message that had been received from space, a message that the experts were unable to verify, at the moment they were checking to see if it was genuine and not some employee inadvertently disrupting the signal by cooking his breakfast in a microwave oven.

After hours of trying to decipher the signal, the astronomers decided to upload the signal to their most powerful computer in the hope it could be analysed. As they waited for the result, they were unaware that the signal from space had converted itself to a computer language that could talk to their mainframe. Within seconds the signal had gained access to the Cloud and had performed an electronic 'handshake' to verify the connection of Earth's computers to the AI housed in the pyramid, on a planet that was located far beyond our solar system.